"Pacer, will you tell me more about your wife?" Colm asked.

"It was a long time ago. After she died, and I left Vietnam—" Pacer paused for a moment. "I don't talk about that time."

"I'm sorry," Colm said. "Pacer—"

"You're so beautiful, Colm," he said, wonder in his voice. She was a magnet that held him fast. Her magic had invaded and swept out the dark corner of his heart. What was her powe Who was she? He'd seen sparks surround he when she grew angry, but she was also vulner-able, and he'd seen tenderness turn her sapphire eyes to velvet.

Pacer suddenly reached out for her, drawing her to him. His mouth covered her sputtering, protesting one. Startled at first, Colm began struggling, but she could not escape him. Then his lips soothed the fight in her, and passion ignited like wildfire.

Feelings raged through Colm she'd never felt before. Anger warred with passion, then anger faded. Flames licked along her veins, melting her resistance. Control fled, desire consumed her, and she was in flames.

Pacer lifted his head for a moment. "Thank you for burying my ghost. . . ."

WHAT ARE *LOVESWEPT* ROMANCES?

They are stories of true romance and touching emotion. We believe those two very important ingredients are constants in our highly sensual and very believable stories in the *LOVESWEPT* line. Our goal is to give you, the reader, stories of consistently high quality that may sometimes make you laugh, sometimes make you cry, but are always fresh and creative and contain many delightful surprises within their pages.

Most romance fans read an enormous number of books. Those they truly love, they keep. Others may be traded with friends and soon forgotten. We hope that each *LOVESWEPT* romance will be a treasure—a "keeper." We will always try to publish

LOVE STORIES YOU'LL NEVER FORGET
BY AUTHORS YOU'LL ALWAYS REMEMBER

The Editors

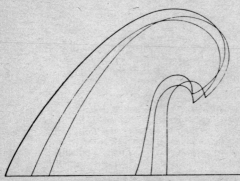

LOVESWEPT® • 341

Helen Mittermeyer
White Heat

 BANTAM BOOKS
NEW YORK • TORONTO • LONDON • SYDNEY • AUCKLAND

WHITE HEAT
A Bantam Book / July 1989

If you would be interested in receiving protective vinyl
covers for your Loveswept books, please write to this address
for information:

Loveswept
Bantam Books
P.O. Box 985
Hicksville, NY 11802

ISBN 0-553-21973-1

Published simultaneously in the United States and Canada

PRINTED IN THE UNITED STATES OF AMERICA

O   0 9 8 7 6 5 4 3 2 1

One

Taking the redhead to bed seemed like the best idea he'd ever had. Would she go for it? Pacer Dillon chuckled to himself. She looked feisty enough to blacken his eye if he propositioned her. But it would be more than worth it if there was a million-to-one chance she would say yes. His blood heated at the thought. Then he told himself he should at least be introduced to her first.

The fierce desire that rushed through him was familiar, yet the uncontrollable urge to get the red-head immediately into his life was alien. Patience, a virtue associated with his American Indian ances-tors, had always been a strong suit with him, but not now. He wanted her. What magic did the lissome creature have?

He studied her closely, admiring her tall, curvy body. Her wild red hair beautifully set off her milk-white skin, and he imagined anger would color those high cheekbones a delicious pink. Her long and silky legs could wrap around a man, body and soul. She was definitely all woman, indubitably sexy, totally irresistible.

Pacer usually took his time with women. Yet staring at this redhead, he couldn't stem his urgency. *Get it together!* he told himself, clenching his teeth in annoyance.

For the first time, he wished he were as smooth as Con or Dev, his friends and business partners. They were happily married men now, who doted on their beautiful wives, but at one time women had gathered around them like bees drawn to honey. Pacer liked women, but he was always reserved, restrained. This sudden desire had thrown him off-balance, out of control. What was it about her that was so compelling? He'd seen her for the first time only half an hour ago.

He strode toward her across the crowded, noisy room. Cocktail parties generally bored him witless. Not this one. The minute he saw her his blue mood had vanished.

He hadn't wanted to come to Houston. The trip had been thrust on him by his two good friends, who hadn't wanted to leave their wives and families. He was here to study in detail a company their corporation was negotiating to purchase. No, he hadn't wanted to come, but now he was considering extending his stay.

He stopped a short distance from the redhead. She was holding court in the center of the two-story living room of the posh apartment, a semicircle of men around her. She was even more beautiful close up—and vibrant. She sent off sparks that sizzled through him.

He was fairly certain this apartment was owned by the redhead and that she was Colm Fitzroy, the woman he had come to see.

His invitation to the party was not from her but from Henry Troy, the executive vice-president of Fitzroy's, the company Pacer and his partners were about to buy. It didn't matter who had invited him. If he hadn't come tonight he might not have met the woman for some time—but he would have met her eventually. He was sure of that. Destiny. The fates were part of his karma.

Perhaps he'd even known her in another lifetime. His strong Creek heritage told him it might be so.

He watched her, watched as she gestured with her champagne glass, a drop or two going over the side. She was slender and small-boned, nearly six feet tall in heels, and perfectly formed. Her neck seemed too fragile to support the heavy fall of fire-red hair that glistened every time she turned her head. He couldn't see her eyes and wondered what color they were. Her derriere was delightfully curved and would fit so nicely into his hands.

If she was Colm Fitzroy, she was smart as well as lovely. She'd been an office manager with two different investment firms before taking over her family's firm after the death of her father, Vince Collamer, earlier that year. Now she was CEO of Fitzroy's. Why she called herself Fitzroy instead of Collamer, Pacer didn't know.

He started toward her again, approaching from behind. The crowd parted when he was only a couple of feet from her. She gestured again with the champagne glass, then stiffened.

Even as he watched, the zipper of her apricot-colored satin cocktail dress began to separate in the middle of her back. She reached back automatically, but only caused the zipper to split more.

Deftly, as though she'd done it countless times, she angled herself so that her back was hidden by an enormous bouquet of flowers on a nearby table.

Pacer continued toward her. With her movement the zipper had split nearly completely, yet she hadn't lost an ounce of composure. He felt an odd ripple of amusement—and more—in his chest. In one long stride he was behind her, his hand closing the gap in her dress. Leaning down, he inhaled her scent. Flowers and what?

"I think you might lose this," he murmured in her ear.

She turned her head slowly and stared up at him, navy-blue eyes widening a fraction as she scanned his face. "Really?" she asked coolly. "You're quite a large safety pin."

He laughed. Her voice was husky, a woodsy sound that ran over his skin like a fragrant breeze. He wanted more. "I wouldn't mind being pinned to you," he said, "but since you aren't wearing a bra and the zipper is still moving, perhaps we'd better retreat." Staring down at her, he thought he would drown in those eyes.

She glanced at the men she'd been talking with. "Shall we back toward that hall? I can go up the rear stairs."

"The choice is yours. By the way, my name is Pacer Creekwood Dillon."

Her brows rose in disbelief. "Is that a stage name? Are you a performer?"

"Are you?"

She studied him for a moment, her eyes narrowed. Then, gracefully, she nodded toward the men and began walking backward. When they reached a short hallway, she said, "You can release me now."

"Are you sure? I'm enjoying holding your . . . zipper." Pacer wasn't sure he could walk away from her. Already the heat of her body seemed a necessity to him, like air or water. His hand tightened on her dress.

"Excuse me," she said, "but I do have to change and get back to my guests."

"Of course."

He released her and watched that intriguing expanse of back as she strode down the hall, then she turned a corner and disappeared. He returned to the living room, taking a drink from a passing attendant, then leaning against a wall.

Colm Fitzroy! he thought. Beautiful, and with a tongue so sharp that talking with her could be a duel. He didn't particularly care for verbal jousting, but she intrigued him, lifted the veil of ennui that had swathed him much of he time lately. He knew he didn't have to stay at this party since he had a meeting scheduled with her the next day. So why didn't he leave? Because Colm Fitzroy was a magnet, drawing him inexorably to her. Who was she really? When had she taken on that hard patina? What enemies had forged the steel he'd seen in her eyes as they'd talked?

He was surprised when she returned to the party quickly, dressed in a cream silk skirt and blouse. She moved slowly around the room, chatting with people, but making her way to the group she'd been talking to when her zipper had broken.

Pushing himself away from the wall, Pacer joined the gathering, listening.

"But Colm," one man said, "how can you make changes like that? Your father would have a heart attack if he even guessed at what you're doing."

Colm, Pacer mused. It was an odd name for a woman. Irish? Welsh? Who had given it to her? He recalled from the information he'd read about her that another person in her family had had the same name. He scanned the faces of the five men standing around her. Were any of them family? Any of them closer than that?

"Vince Collamer's dead," she said slowly, looking directly at each man in turn. "I say who's hired at Fitzroy's now."

"I agree in theory with what you're doing," another man said, "and I think the practice should be augmented, but maybe later. The company's marginal now, Colm. Hiring functional illiterates could tip the balance." The man touched her arm. "I know you've had experience with Caball's and Network, but I think you might be moving too fast."

"It will be my loss, Uncle Henry."

"And mine," Pacer whispered.

Colm's red hair glittered in the light when she swiveled his way, her dark blue eyes assessing him once more. "Yes, I've just associated your name with the offer that came from AbWenDil. No dice, Mr. Dillon." She turned away again.

"Shouldn't we discuss this at a more appropriate time, Ms. Fitzroy?" He'd put a few things together as well. Colm Fitzroy was headstrong—and she was trying to back out of a deal.

"We will, Mr. Dillon, tomorrow at my office. Nine o'clock, the time in the letter." She strode away, her shoulders back and her head high.

"Beautiful, isn't she?" the man she'd called Uncle Henry said. "I'm her executive vice-president, Henry Bellin Troy, and her godfather." The older man with the slightly receding hairline held out his hand. "I was also her father's associate. Glad you could come tonight." He grimaced as he glanced around the room. "Colm is always giving parties. She likes spending money."

"I'm Pacer Dillon, vice-president of AbWenDil Inc."

"I know your name and your company, though it's a new one. That was a pretty formidable group you formed with Conrad Wendel and Deveril Abrams."

Pacer smiled. "Actually we've been partners for some time. Only the corporation's new."

"I saw you and Colm heading for the back hall earlier. Were you ill?"

"Uh . . . no. A minor emergency."

"Oh. I see." Henry Troy frowned as though he didn't see at all.

"About Fitzroy's," Pacer went on. "Until recently it was a very lucrative operation. That doesn't coincide with a conglomerate on the skids now."

"You overheard our conversation."

"And I've been doing a little investigating."

"Fitzroy's has had a few squeaky times since Colm's father died." Henry frowned again. "Vince Collamer was a canny man who played his cards close to the chest. Not even an audit has turned up the real reasons for the dip in liquid assets."

."Intriguing." Pacer's glance slid across the room and fastened on Colm Fitzroy. "I don't usually do business at this kind of affair."

Henry laughed. "Down here we do." He cleared his throat. "I suppose you know that, although we don't consider your bid hostile, we are not that open to accepting it."

"Your books tell us that you could have some bad months facing you. We'd like to deflect that, if possible. We can do it, Mr. Troy, but the options are few and narrowing."

"I know that, but convincing Colm is another story." He exhaled on a half laugh. "When she turned twenty-five she inherited a lion's share of the stock from her mother. That was the deciding factor when the board made her president and CEO after Vince's death, though there was a strong faction against her." Henry frowned fleetingly. "She has a fine business head, but sometimes she's too emotional about Fitzroy's. Sometimes—sometimes it's almost as though she wants to give the entire company away . . . or let it go down the tubes in her effort to rehire employees who were let go in the crunch a couple of years ago."

Pacer continued staring across the room at her, watching as she laughed at something a man said to her. "She has good credentials. Caball's is a tough outfit, and so is Network. She needed a good business background to handle those jobs, and I hear she handled them well." He looked at Henry. "Why the name Colm?"

"She's named for her maternal grandfather."

"I see. No boys in the family?"

"No. Adaira, Colm's mother, was unable to have

any more children." Henry's expression became pensive. "She was as beautiful as Colm."

Pacer studied the other man. "You've known her family a long time then?"

"Colm's mother and I went to the same university, and I knew her in high school."

Pacer saw the tightness in the other man's face and was silent. Henry Bellin Troy reminded him of someone.

Another man approached and began speaking to Henry. Pacer eased away and strolled across the room to a small group gathered around a white piano. Colm was sitting at the piano, running her fingers over the keys.

"Sing, Colm," someone said, and others echoed the request.

Pacer propped himself against a column, forgetting all about Henry Troy as Colm lifted her head and began to sing.

Her husky voice was a silken lariat, reaching out and coiling around him. He shifted, moving his shoulders uncomfortably. It was as though he were being stung from within—as though Colm Fitzroy had entered his blood and were racing through him, taking him, conquering him.

The love ballad was poignant, and when she breathed the last of the lyrics of the song, Pacer could have sworn there was deep pathos in her voice. He was tempted to sweep her up and carry her out of there. Seconds later he was sure he was wrong about the sadness he'd heard, because Colm was laughing and joking with her friends.

He turned away, trying to convince himself to leave,

but something seemed to have chained him to Colm's home. The chattering voices of the other guests irritated him, and he walked out of the living room and down a hall, seeking quiet. The door to a dimly lit room was ajar, and he stepped inside.

Colm had had too much champagne. The party had become like a visit to the dentist, painfully boring. She had a headache. Why the hell did she drink champagne? she asked herself. It always gave her a headache. And why didn't everyone go home?

Trying to smile pleasantly at her guests, she made her way out of the living room and down the hallway to the room that had once been her father's study. She entered it and closed the door.

It no longer looked like Vincent Collamer's room. Colm had seen to that. She had taken her mother's maiden name as soon as she was of age, and she had taken over the family company and her father's home as soon as he had died. She had done her best to eradicate all traces of the man who'd been more of a tormentor than a parent. Vince Collamer had wanted a boy; he'd gotten a girl.

Sinking down in the chair behind the desk, Colm put her head in her hands.

"I guess we both wanted the same thing."

She snapped her head up and stared at the high-backed chair next to the dictionary stand and the man sitting in it. "How did you get in here?" she asked angrily. "Why are you here?"

"Door was open. I wanted some quiet. The country music was getting to me."

"Too bad," she snapped. "That's the kind of music we play down here." When had her father done business with this giant, this craggy mountain man in the Savile Row suit? How tall was he, she wondered. Six four, six five? And he wasn't even from Texas. Was his hair dyed that silver-streaked hue to match his silver-blue eyes? Never.. Besides, he didn't need any artificial additions to his attractiveness. The man literally zinged with sexuality. "I thought I told you the company wasn't for sale," she said.

"I got your letter, Ms. Fitzroy, but our agreement was with Vincent Collamer, the deceased owner of—"

"Fitzroy's belonged to my mother's family. Vince Collamer took it over when he married her."

"And wasn't he your father?"

"Not that it's any business of yours, Mr. Dillon. I took my mother's maiden name when I turned eighteen."

"I see."

"I doubt it. Do you mind leaving this room?"

"May I take you to dinner?"

"What? When?" His abrupt question had her sputtering, and that irked her. He made her fumble, threw her off stride. "I came in here because I have a headache and—"

"You don't have it now," he drawled. "Your tantrum wiped it out."

Inhaling deeply, Colm readied herself to take him down a peg or two. Then she blinked, realizing that the headache *was* gone. It lessened her anger a tad. "Where did you want to go to dinner?" she asked. "*If* we were going, which we're not."

"Roget's."

She stared at him. "Where's that? It must be new."

"Off Fifth Avenue, not far from Central Park."

"What? Manhattan? New York?"

"Do you do that all the time?"

"What?"

"Ask questions in response to questions, never answering anything."

Colm jumped to her feet and glared at him. It shook her when he languidly pushed himself from the chair and walked over to her. Few men stood inches taller than she, but this man did. "We have a meeting at nine in the morning," she muttered, feeling extremely out of sorts.

"We can have it in New York."

"The answer is no to your business proposition. Fitzroy's is not for sale to you or anyone else."

"How about dinner?"

She stared up at his handsome face. Heat was coming off him. His innocent look was bogus. He was like a charcoal fire at its hottest, apparently harmless but lethal. White heat!

"No more questions?" he asked.

His lazy drawl seemed to scrape over her skin, raising goose bumps. This was no Texas gentleman. "Where are you from?"

"Ah, there are more questions." He moved closer to the desk.

Colm felt crowded. She sat back down in the desk chair. "You have a touch of Texas in your voice."

"Oklahoma. I was born in a cabin on a ranch thirty miles outside of nowhere. I think the place is dust now."

"Your people ran cattle?"

"No. I was orphaned young," he said easily, "and I broke horses and cleaned stables."

"Touching."

He grinned. "You don't believe me."

"I've read about you, Mr. Dillon. You graduated from Princeton summa cum laude and you have a master's degree in business."

"So do you."

She blinked. "You've done a check on me."

"The regular business check. I read it on the flight down here. Impressive background."

"I see."

"I think you must have been a dynamite model."

"I was," she said tartly. Talking to him was like being on a teeter-totter, she thought. Up, then down, up, then down. Damn the man. He threw curves and spitballs. Weren't spitballs illegal? She'd bet anything he'd been a street fighter in his childhood, ranch or no ranch. Men were usually so easy to read and handle. Only her father had been difficult— and now this one. She would have no truck with men like that. "I won't change my mind on the company."

Pacer shrugged. "Neither will we. Our company had a firm verbal agreement, Ms. Fitzroy."

"I'm not selling."

"We'll take you to court."

"Try it. I have lawyers too."

He nodded. "I'll see you at nine in the morning."

"You could leave tonight, Mr. Dillon. I won't change my mind."

His slow smile made her breathing constrict, her scalp prickle with alarm.

"Business isn't the only magnet in Houston, Ms. Fitzroy."

When he left the room, Colm stayed where she was, breathing deeply, trying to steady herself. She hadn't drunk that much champagne, yet she couldn't calm her pounding heart. Pacer Creekwood Dillon had taken all the oxygen in the room with him. Was he perhaps not from Manhattan but from another planet? If so, he wasn't even a friendly alien.

Pacer left the party and returned to his hotel. He made two phone calls, one to cancel his afternoon flight for the next day and the other to the offices of AbWenDil. He left a message on the machine explaining that wrapping up the deal was going to take some time and that he'd call again in a day or so.

After he hung up the phone, he restlessly paced his suite. He knew what he wanted—Colm Fitzroy. It would be easy enough to take care of the sexual urge, but he wanted only Colm, a volatile, beautiful creature who didn't seem drawn to him at all. Hell, she'd hated him on sight because he wanted her company! What had forged that intense drive in her that was part anger and part fear? He had felt it strongly. Knowing what caused it was swiftly becoming a prime concern.

Irritation laced with black humor assailed him. How many times had he chuckled at the way his friends, Dev Abrams and Con Wendel, doted on their women, how they were mesmerized by them, how their days were colored by them?

Was Colm weaving her magic around him? Though

the sensation was new to him, he had an inkling that was what was building in him. Colm Fitzroy was fashioning a net around him and he wasn't even struggling.

Shrugging his shoulders as though he could shake off her power, he went into the bathroom and ran the cold water in the shower. He might need a bath in ice cubes before the night was over. Colm Fitzroy was very sexually alive in his mind. Sleep would be a long time coming. Damn her!

Two

Fitzroy's was an incredibly successful investment banking organization. The building that housed it stood proud among its peers in Houston's business community, its glass and steel facade giving it the look of a giant harmonica. Glittering in the strong Texas sunshine, it was like a shrine to the money and power it represented.

For Texas, Fitzroy's was old money. Caleb Fitzroy had come west with a carpetbag, a bowler hat, and an agile mind, buying up dusty plots of ground that no one wanted. Oil had turned the land to gold. Caleb had chuckled up his sleeve and rubbed his rabbit foot. Good fortune followed good fortune.

He married well, had a wonderful son named Colm who'd turned an even more agile mind to the business. Through Adaira's time the company flourished. Only in the last ten years had there been problems.

As always when Colm parked in the underground parking garage in the slot reserved for the chief executive, she shuddered. Not all the memories of her father had been erased. Exorcising them was difficult, but by slowly hiring back all the old employees, widening the scope of the company, refocusing the goals, she would, step by step, win.

She got out of her car and turned toward the elevator that would take her from the garage directly to the executive office. When a shadow separated itself from a concrete stanchion, she paused warily. Then the figure stepped into the light and she gasped. "You! How did you get in here?"

"Easily," Pacer said.

"No, it wouldn't be. We have security."

"You need to beef it up," he told her softly. "Shall we go up?" He crooked his arm.

Ignoring the gesture, Colm swept by him. "You're thirty minutes early. I have mail to go through before the meeting."

"I'll help you."

"No thanks." Colm jabbed her key into the lock for the elevator. Her dreams had been colored by Pacer Creekwood Dillon. And now he turned up in her parking garage. Damn the man!

When the elevator doors slid open, she stepped into the air-conditioned interior.

Pacer was right behind her. "That peach color suits you. Wear it when we have dinner."

"No."

"All right. Wear something else."

Once more his benign smile made her shiver. It was like a pretty flower trying to hide the mouth of a volcano, an ineffectual effort to mask ferocious power.

"Cold?" He moved closer and wrapped a strong arm around her. "Better?"

"No—yes. I'm not cold." she tried to free herself but couldn't budge him. Looking up at him, she glared. She was used to gazing straight into men's eyes. Pacer Dillon was too tall. "Let me go."

"I don't know if I can."

"What?" she felt her body freeze—and then somehow melt.

"I want to keep you warm."

"I always thought Indian men were polite."

"We are."

"Then release me."

"Keep me warm, darlin'."

His caressing tone turned her knees to water. "No need."

"I love that rusty sound to your voice. It sends shivers up my spine."

"That sometimes happens just before I blacken someone's eye."

"I'll remember to duck."

The elevator doors slid open quietly. Most of the employees were already at their desks working.

Colm wriggled free. "Look, Mr. Dillon, I—"

"You shouldn't raise your voice that way. They might think you're upset." He nodded toward the staff.

"What?" She turned around to see several people watching them. Pacer took her arm and led her from the elevator.

"Nice executive offices," he said politely.

"So happy you approve."

"Have another headache? You're talking through your teeth."

"Mr. Dill-on!"

Heads turned in the secretarial area.

"They're looking at us again," Pacer said blandly. "That's why you should have an elevator that opens directly into your office."

"What?" She scowled at Pacer. "Oh, go away, will you?"

Head high, she stalked through the long line of desks to the private corridor that led to her office. Opening the door, she stormed into the outer office and glared at her secretary. "Jane! No calls."

"Ah, right, Ms. Fitzroy." Jane was staring over Colm's shoulder, her eyes wide. "Someone's at your back, though."

"Get rid of him."

"Me? No, ma'am. I'd want danger pay for that." Jane smiled.

"Coward," Colm muttered, frowning at her normally efficient secretary. Jane was positively drooling.

"Yes, ma'am. How do," she said to Pacer, her Houston drawl pronounced. "I'm Jane Sethwaite."

"Howdy. I'm Pacer Creekwood Dillon."

"That's a right pretty name."

"Jane!"

"Yes, ma'am. Bye, Mr. Dillon, sir."

"Don't worry about me, Jane. I'll just take a chair and wait for my appointment. Do you have coffee? I haven't had breakfast this morning."

"Oh, my. That's the most important meal of the day." Jane jumped to her feet and rushed from the office.

"Jane!" Colm looked after her secretary, who was scampering down the hall.

"Cool down," Pacer said. "All that steam will blow your head off."

She gripped a paperweight on Jane's desk. "I do not blow my top."

"Let me help," he said, eyeing the paperweight warily. "Is this the mail?"

"No. Yes. Don't touch that. What are you doing?"

"You're doing it again."

"Doing what?" Colm could've bitten her tongue through.

"Talking like an M-1 rifle. Firing questions like ammunition. You have a habit of doing that."

"You said I asked too many questions, Mr. Dillon. Make up your mind." Would she never learn not to snap at his bait?

"That, too."

"I don't have time for this."

"Don't grind your teeth that way. Your dental bills must be high."

"Mr. Dillon, if you please—"

"Talking rapid-fire doesn't fit your Southern image. That's not Texan, little lady. Shall we go in?" He pushed open the door to her inner office, gesturing for her to precede him.

"You are undermining my staff," she said, stalking past him. What had happened to the cool attitude she'd been able to maintain with everyone else? How had Pacer Dillon gotten past her protective shield? She would ignore him, pretend he wasn't in her office. She sat down at her desk and began pulling files from her briefcase.

Pacer hitched one hip up onto a corner of her desk. "Do you look like the great Colm Fitzroy who founded this business empire?"

Colm had fully intended to ignore him, but mention of her beloved grandfather broke down her fences. "I guess I do. My uncle says my mother told people that I did."

Pacer caught the wistful smile.

"Some even say I'm like his father, Caleb Fitzroy."

"A wily old thief, as I recall."

Colm laughed, but she studied him with new eyes. "In a way I'm a maverick too. I'm the only one in the family with the color eyes I have."

"Navy-blue sapphires," he murmured, gazing into those eyes. Was Colm Fitzroy becoming an obsession?

Colm stood and walked to the far wall, switching on a portrait light to illuminate two paintings. "This is Great-Grandfather Caleb and Grandfather Colm. "My mother, Adaira Fitzroy, was the heir to all they had. Now it's mine and I won't sell." Colm whirled to face him. "And I will fight you in court every inch of the way."

He shrugged. "That's your prerogative."

The door opened and Jane walked into the office carrying a silver tray. She beamed at Pacer. "I have fresh squeezed orange and grapefruit juice, warm croissants, butter curls, and jam here. Along with coffee and cups, of course. Will that do?"

"It's wonderful, Jane. What a treasure you are." He took the tray from her, smiling. "Thank you."

"You're welcome, Mr. Dillon."

When the door closed behind Jane, Pacer turned to Colm. "Join me?"

"No. I rarely eat in the morning."

He set the tray on a round table in front of a semicircular couch. Then he walked across the room to Colm and scooped her up in his arms. "It won't hurt you to have some juice and a croissant."

She stared blankly at him. "Put me down."

"I will, darlin', as soon as I reach the couch." He edged around the table and sat down with Colm in his lap. "This is nice."

She tried to wriggle free, but he tightened his arms around her.

"I have to tell you, darlin'," he drawled, "that wonderful movement you're making with that gorgeous backside is having an effect on me."

"What?" She straightened, her spine ramrod stiff. "Let me up."

"Only if you insist. I like the sensation."

"You are here for business, Mr. Dillon."

"Your voice drives me wild." He kissed her ear, then lifted her off his lap and set her down next to him. "Drink this," he said, pouring her a glass of orange juice. "We all need vitamin C."

"You're not a doctor." She sipped the icy juice, letting it cool her throat.

"I'd like to take care of you," he said softly.

She gazed closely at him. "Why did you frown just then?"

He poured two cups of coffee and shrugged. "I'm not used to the feeling, darlin'. The only women I cherish are married to friends of mine. I love them dearly."

A sharp pain had Colm gasping. Why should it bother her if he had dozens of women? she asked herself. He was nothing to her. She gulped more juice. It caught in the back of her throat and she coughed.

"Swallow the wrong way?" he asked, patting her back.

"Stop that." Colm inhaled deeply, then took the piece of buttered croissant he handed her.

Neither said anything else as they finished the light meal.

"Now, doesn't that feel better?" Pacer asked after draining his coffee cup.

"You sound like a nanny."

"Testy again? Need an aspirin?"

"I don't have a headache and—"

The door opened and Jane stuck her head in. "Meeting's in five minutes, ma'am."

"Good Lord. I have notes to look at." Colm jumped to her feet.

Pacer walked alongside her to the desk. "Can I help you?"

"No. You're the enemy, trying to move in on my company."

"That's not true. We had a bona fide response to our offer, Colm, and you know it. It was made in front of your lawyers and ours."

"I will not sell and risk my people being tossed out on the street again because of an austerity program. I know and you know that the first order of the day when stripping a company is to 'disengage the personnel,' to put it in the cliché terms of a hostile takeover."

"There is no evidence of a hostile takeover in our bid. You've read the prospectus, what we plan to do . . ."

"And you know that many a shady deal is couched in sweet legalese." She bit her lip as she watched his rough-hewn features harden, those silver-blue eyes narrow and turn metallic.

"We're not crooks, Ms. Fitzroy. We don't have to be."

"I wasn't taking shots at you—"

"You were."

She took a deep breath, her chin lifting. "It doesn't matter. I won't sell. This company is mine and I intend that the people associated with Fitzroy's will get what is due them."

"From the statements I've seen, you seem to consider Chapter Eleven bankruptcy a viable course for doing this."

Angered by his implicit criticism, she snapped, "You don't speak like any Oklahoma wrangler I've known."

"I'm Creek on my mother's side and very proud of it. And incidentally, my father was very proud of my mother's lineage, too, and he was full-blooded Irish. And they were both proud of what they did."

"That sounded crass and small-minded. I didn't mean it that way." She pushed at the few tendrils of hair that had escaped from her chignon.

"Apology accepted. Why are you heading your company into bankruptcy?"

"I've never seen an Indian with silvery eyes and hair."

"No? Then you'll be pleased to know that my cousins are dark. Now tell me why you're trying to destroy your company."

"I'm not!" Stung, she wanted to strike him, hard. She resisted and began gathering papers for the meeting, stuffing them into her briefcase. "I believe in justice."

"And the American Way. You sound like a recruiting poster."

"Don't you believe in justice, Mr. Dillon?"

"Yes, but I'm a businessman. I don't believe in kamikaze fiscal practices."

Colm leaned forward across the desk, bracing her

fists on top of it. Her knuckles whitened. "Get out of here. And take your damned hostile takeover bid with—"

The door opened again. "D'yall know you're late for the meeting?" Jane asked.

"Damn!" Colm spun around and grabbed for her briefcase, throwing herself off-balance. She staggered, the swivel chair rocking as she grabbed for it, then she was falling.

"Gotcha," Pacer whispered, lifting her in his arms, his mouth close to her ear. "Stop struggling."

"My goodness, he's strong, isn't he, Ms. Fitzroy?" Jane said dreamily.

"Put me down," Colm said through her teeth. He did, so hard it jarred her. "Beast."

"You said to put you down, ma'am," he drawled. "Tell me why you don't have a Texas accent, ma'am."

"None of your business."

"She went to school in the East, that's why," Jane said, her gaze glued to Pacer.

"Thank you, Jane." He grinned at Colm. "Shall we go to the meeting?"

She stormed ahead of him out the door, glaring at Jane, who was still staring vapidly at Pacer.

The special meeting of the board seemed to erupt with Colm's opening statement that she was not going to sell Fitzroy's to AbWenDil. Though her vice-presidents tried to support her, many of the board members were very interested in what Pacer had to say in rebuttal.

The upshot of two hours of wrangling was a stalemate.

Pacer followed Colm from the boardroom. "Have dinner with me."

"No." She swung around to face him. "I have work to do, Mr. Dillon. Fighting takeovers takes time and energy. Excuse me."

"Of course." He watched her stride down the hall, her stiffness in no way detracting from the sensuality of her body. "You are too beautiful, Colm Fitzroy," he murmured, half entranced, half irritated.

He returned to his hotel and found several messages for him from Dev Abrams. He dialed the office in New York. "Dev? What are you doing in town? Nothing wrong, is there?"

"Nothing. In fact, Felicity and I will be going back to the mountains in a couple of days. My lady is bothered by the heat."

"Pregnancy can do that." Pacer chuckled. "I thought two was enough for you."

"It was for me. Felicity has a mind of her own."

Pacer could hear the concern behind the light humor in his friend's voice. "Take it easy, Dev. Felicity's in wonderful health."

"And I want to keep her that way. Hang on a sec. Con's here in my office. I'll put you on the speaker phone."

After a moment Pacer heard Con's voice. "What's going on? Why the delay? Did you find the girl of your dreams in Houston?"

Silence.

"Pace?" Dev asked sharply.

"Tell us," Con demanded.

"Colm Fitzroy is quite a woman and she hates me," Pacer drawled. "Bad beginning. Stop laughing, you jackasses."

"I love it," Dev said. "He sounds like he's in our boat now, Con."

"So he does, Dev, so he does."

"She won't sell," Pacer interjected when he could.

"What? She has to sell. We have a firm commitment."

"Sorry, she's going to fight us."

"Bring her to New York, Pace. Let us talk to her. Our expense. Invite her to tear up Manhattan."

"I don't know if she'd be that impressed, Dev. The lady is one of a kind."

Con chuckled. "Then we would understand her, since that's what we married."

"Yeah, I'm beginning to understand what drove you two. I don't like it."

"It ain't easy," Dev said.

"Bring her up here, Pacer."

"I don't think she'll come."

"Well, give it a try."

"We'll see."

Colm worked like a wild woman for the rest of the day. She accomplished a great deal, yet no matter how she drowned herself in statistics and figures, she couldn't quite banish Pacer Creekwood Dillon from her mind.

Other men she'd found interesting, even intriguing, but she'd always been in control. As a child she'd decided that when she was able she would handle her own life, and no man would run her or manipulate her. There hadn't been a time that she hadn't been managing her own affairs since she'd gotten her first job at sixteen.

She had fought hard to break away from the restraints of her father. Vince Collamer had always been in control of everything and everyone he touched.

When his daughter had started to balk, he'd increased the pressure, never letting her forget he would have preferred a son and she would never be good enough. In a way it had been good training to fight with her father. It had taught her much about surviving in the business world.

Colm had developed an ability to separate feelings from goals, to plot her life toward achieving a purpose. A determination to be her own person no matter what the cost had become her raison d'être very early in the game. And she'd succeeded. Her degrees in business had been buttressed by jobs with two well-known companies. Though others had been sure she would work for Fitzroy's when she completed her MBA, Colm had found it challenging and rewarding to work for the other firms. When she had taken over at Fitzroy's after her father's death, she found those other working experiences stood her in good stead.

Pacer Creekwood Dillon was not going to throw any glitches in the works. She wouldn't let him.

Pacer Creekwood Dillon had taken all her preconceived notions about men, all her in-control feelings and dumped them out the window. Damn him!

He was smooth—but rough. He was sophisticated—but country. He was Ivy League—but backwoods. Who was he? What was he? Did anyone know? No! She wouldn't think of him. There was work to be done.

When Colm finally lifted her head, Jane and the rest of the staff were long gone.

Stretching, she reached for her briefcase and stifled a yawn.

When the elevator came, she propped her tired

body against the wall and rode down to the garage with her eyes shut. She stepped out into the dimly lit parking area and started toward her car. When she heard a rustling sound she stiffened. It was a security man, wasn't it? Recalling what Pacer Dillon had said about "beefing up security" she continued cautiously toward her car. Instinct made her muscles tighten, readying for fight or flight.

Suddenly strong hands came down on her shoulders. "Don't be afraid," Pacer said.

Shaken, she stared up at him. "You scared me."

"Sorry."

They stood together, not speaking, their breathing the only sound in the almost empty garage.

"I didn't mean to startle you," he said. "Are you all right?"

"You do move quietly." Pacer Creekwood Dillon was an enigma, a rather frightening one.

"Why don't we go back to my hotel, let me wash up, then we'll talk over dinner?"

She hesitated. "All right. My car's here." Why had she said that? He was the enemy. On the other hand, maybe she should get to know her adversary better.

"Do you prefer a particular type of food?" he asked. Delight poured through him because he was going to be with her.

"We can eat at my place. My housekeeper will have left something." *Damn*, she thought. Her insanity was worsening.

"Sounds great," Pacer murmured, taking her arm, liking the feel of her.

He kept his hand on her arm as they approached her car, looking around him all the while. "Security should have spot-checked through here by now, but I've seen no one."

"Cautious, aren't you."

"Very."

They reached her car, and she unlocked the doors.

"Do you want me to drive?" he asked.

"I'll drive. Tell me which hotel, then tell me why you're so suspicious." She headed toward the ramp, up and out to the street.

Pacer admired the way she handled the car, driving fast, yet smoothly, expertly. "You had a good teacher."

She smiled. "My uncle Henry taught me. And my other uncle, Rance Caleb, used to let me drive his pickup all over the ranch. . . ."

Her voice trailed off, and Pacer studied her carefully. What ranch? There'd been pain in her voice when she'd spoken of it. He pondered the beautiful woman next to him and wondered why the least nuance in her life was important to him.

"Tell me why you're so suspicious," she said.

"Instinct . . . background . . . experience." He shrugged.

Colm nodded but didn't answer him. She understood the need to be careful. There had been a few times—but better not to think of those. The last few years had been pretty good.

Pacer's hotel wasn't far from the Galleria, and the drive was quick.

"I'll be right out," he said as she pulled up to the doors. "Unless you'd like to accompany me inside."

"I'll wait here."

"Hey, I like that smile. Do it again."

"Hurry, or I'll take off."

"Be back before you miss me."

"That could be a while."

She shivered when he laughed, then watched as he walked rapidly into the tall building. He was quick and quiet. As big as he was, he'd been able to get into the security-controlled garage at Fitzroy's with ease. Should she "beef up security," as he had phrased it? Tomorrow she would call Chalmers, head of security, and talk to him.

Even Jane thought Pacer Dillon was special, Colm mused, and he was. His craggy looks would break hearts wherever he went. Had he said he was married? She felt a pain in her chest and told herself it was indigestion.

Colm closed her eyes and shook her head. He wasn't for her. She had laid out a road for herself, and she was going to follow it. But what a hunk of masculinity Pacer Dillon was. Would it hurt to spend an evening with him? She could use a little diversion. And she couldn't deny the sexual charge that crackled between them whenever they were together. Each time he touched her she had to struggle not to melt into his arms. If he kissed her . . .

"Daydreaming?"

Her eyes flew open and she saw him standing beside the car. "It's evening," she said hoarsely, forcing her errant thoughts away.

"So it is." He slid into the car, his arm touching hers. She couldn't help flinching at the sudden heat that shot through her.

"You were fast," she said, looking at him sideways. Dressed in jeans and a beige polished cotton shirt, he looked casually elegant. Which face of Dillon's was the real one?

"I took the stairs."

She noticed that he didn't even seem to be out of breath. "If you'd fallen down those stairs, we would have had to spend the evening in the hospital." Checking that she was clear, she pulled out onto the road.

"Not a hospital. Not a chance."

Catching the harshness in his voice, she looked at him for a second. "Why do you hate hospitals so much?" She sensed a pulling away, a stiffening, though he didn't actually move.

"I was in Vietnam," he said abruptly.

"Wounded? Is that why you don't like them?"

"Partly. I was a patient a few times."

She hesitated, wondering why it was suddenly important that she know more about this man. But whatever the reason, she had to know. "Tell me," she said.

"I helped to run a hospital for a while with a woman doctor," he said in a flat voice, staring straight ahead. "We took in the street children in Saigon, and there were plenty of them."

"Just the two of you cared for all those children?"

"Sometimes we had help. My buddies brought food. When the Americans left Saigon, I had plenty of avenues for getting supplies."

"But something happened."

"There was still sporadic fighting after the Americans left. A shell hit the gas stove in the kitchen. The whole place exploded. . . ." His voice died.

"The children? The doctor?"

"Yes."

"And you were close to the doctor?"

"She was my wife."

"Oh. I am sorry."

"Thank you." Pacer couldn't believe he'd told her so much. Even Con and Dev weren't quite sure he'd married. He hadn't been able to talk about Marya, part French, part Vietnamese, and all beautiful. Now he'd spilled it out to Colm.

"You don't talk about it much, do you?" she asked.

"No."

"And you've never married again?"

"No."

Colm's hands tightened on the steering wheel. She could feel his pain, his sorrow. It sliced through her and joined her own ache of rejection that had come with the knowledge that the pale-haired giant of an Indian had been very much in love—and maybe was still. "I'm sorry for your loss," she murmured.

"It was a long time ago."

Pacer looked out the side window, not seeing the bright lights of Houston. He was shaken because for the first time since he'd returned from the Far East, he wasn't able to call up Marya's face. She was deeply imbedded in his heart for all time, but the pain was gone now, and he could put her to rest. The rage that had consumed him at first had abated over the years, yet still simmered. It surprised and unsettled him to find it gone. In its place . . .

Marya had been a wonder who had given him peace and joy—not the rough, alien force that Colm Fitzroy unleashed in him. Being with her sparked facets of barbarity and gentleness unknown to him.

He wasn't used to being off-balance. Years of self-determination and an iron will had fine-honed his perceptions of himself, his goals, even his dreams. He structured his life carefully, allowing some in to share it, but closing out most. That was his chosen way. Control of self, of future, of his life. Control! But not with Colm Fitzroy. She rocked him. He didn't like it.

He turned to gaze at her as she parked in the garage underneath her apartment building. She was a magnet who held him. Her magic had invaded and swept out a few dark corners of his heart. What was her power? Who was she? Strongly beautiful, with angles and lines accentuating the curves. Tough, resilient—and when angry she fired the air around her with blue sparks. She wasn't soft and tractable, yet beneath it all she was vulnerable, and he'd seen tenderness turn those sapphire eyes to velvet.

How many depths were there to Colm Fitzroy? He wanted to discover and enter those mysterious hideaways in her soul.

Reaching out for her, he lifted her over the console and into his lap. His mouth covered her sputtering, protesting one.

Too startled at first, Colm finally began to struggle, but it was to no avail. The hard arms encasing her were like steel. Then she forgot to fight him as his mouth worked its magic on her.

The kiss went on and on, his hard mouth against her soft one, lips urging lips apart, tongues dueling and jousting. Passion rose like a tidal wave, swamping them both.

Feelings raged through Colm that she'd never felt before. Anger and passion warred, then anger faded. Fire licked along her veins, fanning heat through her system and melting all before it. No emotions were left except the smoldering wants, desires, and needs that she hadn't even been aware she possessed. Control fled. Desire consumed. Pacer Creek-wood Dillon was white heat, and he'd set her on fire.

Pacer lifted his head for a moment. "Thanks for burying my ghost." Then his mouth was on hers again and the fire flared anew.

Colm heard him through a fog. What did he mean? What ghost? Her mind fought her feelings. Stay free! Fight the attraction! Passion wasn't for her. These sensations were to be controlled.

All the mental demands went flying as the tumultuous emotions swept them away. Swamped, enveloped, whisked into the strange and wonderful vortex, Colm was mute, in awe.

"Darlin'," Pacer murmured. "You're so beautiful."

"Hungry." Foggy, out of sync, she grabbed for the mundane lifeline. "Dinner."

"You're out of breath." Pacer's mind was aflame with all the new sensations. He wanted her, yet a fierce need to protect her from even one bruise tumbled alongside the desire to shake her for stealing his control.

"I'm in training," she muttered. Her eyelids felt as though they were weighted with lead. "Have to go." Dillon must have been on the FBI's most wanted list, she thought. He was number one!

"All right." Touching her was a sweet agony. His libido was already in overdrive.

When he slid her across his lap to let her out the passenger door, she could not mistake his arousal.

"See how you set me on fire, Colm Fitzroy."

"Overactive glands," she said.

"It might be a little more than that."

"Time to eat." Her feet hit the concrete and she wasn't sure her shaky legs would support her. She felt disheveled in mind and body, completely out of kilter. Pacer Creekwood Dillon secreted a dangerous drug in his lips. Insanity, thy name is Colm Fitzroy!

Pressing the elevator button she stared at the closed doors as though she could will them open.

"You're liable to press your finger through the wall, darlin'."

"I'm not your darling."

"I think you are."

She swiveled her head his way. "And that angers you, doesn't it? Too bad, mister." Glee pushed past the anger she'd been feeling toward herself. For a moment she was heady with power that he'd been caught in the web of sensuality just as she had.

It was a fleeting victory. She'd been able to throw Pacer Creekwood Dillon off-balance, but at no small cost to the self-control that meant so much to her. Who was he anyway? Seeing safer conversational ground, she raced for it. "How is it that I've heard of your partners, read about them, but you're such a mystery man?"

"Not to the people who matter to me." He took her arm as they entered the elevator, keeping her close to his body. "You matter to me," he told her softly.

Her knees turned to water and she would have sunk to the floor if Pacer hadn't been holding her. "You're crowding me."

"And you're squeaking."

"I don't do that."

"Just for me?"

"No!"

"No need to shout, darlin'. I can hear you." He leaned down and kissed her earlobe, his tongue feathering over the sensitive skin.

The elevator doors opened and she jumped out into the small hall with three doors opening off it. Putting her key in the lock in the center door, she couldn't quite still the tremors in her hand.

"This is very nice," Pacer said. "I didn't look at it properly last night."

"Thank you. From what my uncles tell me, my mother had a hand in designing this building. She was quite clever."

"Like mother, like daughter." He followed her into the apartment and looked around the foyer, admiring the marble floors, the wainscoted walls. "This looks much like a Manhattan apartment. It's very appealing now that people aren't cluttering it."

Colm's heart jerked erratically. The man was a damned seducer. "When I first moved in, it was very western looking," she said crisply. "I like the changes the decorators made."

"It was your father's place first."

"Actually it's the firm's. This building is owned by Fitzroy's. At one time we owned the ranch where I was born, but it was sold."

Pacer scanned her tight features, seeing the thinly veiled anger. "And that's a thorn in your side."

"That ranch was my heritage, not to be sold." She inhaled a deep, shaken breath. "I've tried to buy it back twice, but I've been outbid." She saw a lazy smile spread across Pacer's face. "What are you thinking?"

"That you didn't have the right bidder, darlin'. Tell me where this property is and let me have a go."

"It wouldn't do any good. Some friends of my father's own it now and they have no desire to sell."

"Where is it?" Pacer took a pad from his hip pocket, his brow cocked questioningly.

She described an area to the west of Houston. "But there's nothing you can do. I've talked to lawyers and judges about this."

"I'm sure you have." He jotted down the address of the big Texas spread. "These are almost dinosaurs now, aren't they?"

"There are still some big ranches. Not as large as the King Ranch maybe, but there are still some imposing places across Texas and some of the other southwestern states." She walked toward the back of the apartment, very aware of Pacer at her side. "The ranch that belonged to the Fitzroys was a big employer of people in that area, many of them third-generation employees." Her lips tightened. "The new owners have let most of them go." She whirled to face him. "That's wrong and that's one of the reasons I'm going to fight your takeover. Some of the people who've been let go at Fitzroy's were second and third generation. They depended on Fitzroy's for survival."

"I'm not your enemy, darlin'. Neither are my partners."

"No? Then go back to Manhattan and rescind your offer."

"I can't do that."

"I see." She turned her back on him, her hands curling into fists.

"It isn't just us you resent. You're angry because you have no control over how things are done at the ranch. Am I right?"

She faced him once more, her face flushed, and she swallowed hard. "Many of the people who are out of work and struggling to feed their families have been friends of my family for generations. Should I be unaffected by their plight?" She bit her lip when her voice quavered.

"No. You're a beautiful, caring woman." Pacer leaned down and kissed the tip of her nose. "A very lovable trait."

The world tipped, shuddered, then settled back. Colm's being trembled as though she stood on a precipice, readying herself for a dive into the unknown. Pacer Dillon was like lava, rolling over her, overwhelming her.

Moving away from him, she took a casserole dish from the refrigerator and placed it in the microwave. "I thought I'd get over it, learn to deal with it . . . and I have to some extent. But many things rankle. It was my birthright." She was mad, she thought, to open her soul to a stranger!

"And you think your father was cavalier in selling it?"

"Yes."

"Have you considered the hard times that the oil and real estate businesses down here have gone through in the last ten years?"

"Yes, actually I have." She lifted her chin. "I've seen the Fitzroy books. We have had reversals, but not the kind that needed the money from the sale of Boru."

Pacer straightened, whistling softly. "Boru belonged to Fitzroy's? That's news to me. My friends have purchased fine breeding stock from that ranch."

She smiled tremulously. "Some of the best Arabian mix breeds in the world. With judicious breeding we developed a horse second to none for speed and endurance, not to mention intelligence and beauty."

He nodded. "So I've heard."

The microwave buzzer sounded loud and intrusive, and Colm jumped as though stung. "I'll get the fixings for the salad, and our dinner will be ready in a few minutes."

"What is it?"

"Shrimp barbecue, one of my favorites."

"Sounds good."

They were quiet as they set the table in the small eating nook off the kitchen. After Colm had served the food she sat down. She shivered when Pacer pulled his chair around so that he was next to her and not across from her.

"Umm, this is good," he said after sampling the food. "So's the salad. You have a wonderful cook."

"Pina is the daughter of the woman who took care of my mother. She worked at the ranch house at one time with her sister. . . ." Colm shook her head and said no more.

"Maybe we could take a picnic out to the ranch tomorrow. Could you take a long lunch break?"

"It's a good distance," she said, smiling at the thought of seeing her home again. "We'd have to fly."

"I can get a chopper—and fly it too."

She nodded. "All right. There's a helipad on the ranch. I haven't been out there in a while myself." All at once it was very important to her to have Pacer see the place of her birth. "We could do that."

"Fine. Then maybe on the way I could convince you to join me in New York for a week or so." He held up his hand when she started to speak. "Don't tell me how busy you are. Everyone is. But I think you owe it to your company to check out our offer, Colm. And on our home ground. It's not a hostile attempt . . . but I know there will be some in the near future. Your situation is prime for a hostile takeover, and I think you know that. Fiscally you're rocky enough that if someone did make a hard run at you, you could cave in, then you would have no strength to play from, a dead hand. Your liquidity has been dented, and it wouldn't take much to deplete it totally."

"I understand what you're saying. I do. But . . . I have to fight this my way. This company has been in my mother's family for many years. It's been the mainstay employer to hundreds of families who have been loyal to it. I won't have them cut out just to make money."

"We have no thought of paring the business, Colm. We want to expand, not extract the liquid assets and run." He leaned toward her. "Come to New York as our guest and we'll show you the stats. Bring whomever you choose as your personal expert."

She hesitated. "That seems fair."

"It is. Bring your executive vice-president."

"It might be just the thing for Uncle Henry. He's never had any family but the company. His wife died just before I was born and he never married again."

Pacer sat back in his chair, balancing it on two legs. "There you are. What could be fairer?"

"Nothing." she smiled, caught in a reverie. "When I was at Sarah Lawrence, I stayed at the Plaza Hotel one weekend. It was marvelous."

"You could stay at my place. It's big enough."

"No. I think the Plaza would be fine. I could show my uncle Central Park, and I could jog."

"I'll come with you. It's better to have company when you do that."

"We're not there yet," she said, and laughed, feeling more carefree than she had in months.

They finished their dinner and cleared the dishes, rinsing them and putting them into the dishwasher.

"I should really get to bed," Colm said, turning to him. "If we're going on a picnic I should get to the office early." She held out her hand to Pacer.

He took her hand and tugged gently. She stumbled forward into his arms. "I need your mouth, not your hand, darlin'."

"I'm not your darling," she said dizzily before she was spun off the planet by Pacer Dillon's power. Her hands dug into his waist and she clung to him. To hell with sanity! He was warm and wonderful.

Three

"You do fly well."

"Thank you, ma'am. Where do I land?"

Colm pondered that. "I know the people who own the ranch," she said finally. "As I told you, they're friends of my father's, but I can't say I'm really close to them. Let's not use the helipad; let's land to the north of the property, right past that ridge. Okay? That land belongs to Rance Caleb. He used to run the ranch for my grandfather." She grinned. "He's one of my godfather's buddies, and he used to cover up for me when I got into trouble."

"Which was a good share of the time, no doubt."

"I'll bet I was an angel compared to you."

He smiled slowly. "Could be."

She laughed, and the sound seemed to run over Pacer's skin like quick, sweet kisses.

"I love that sound," he said. "Kiss me, then get ready for the landing."

"I think that's a contradiction in terms," she murmured. Why kiss him just because he suggested it? she asked herself. Did he think she was a fool? Leaning forward she pressed her mouth to his, stifling the practical voice that told her she *was* a fool.

Pacer lifted his head reluctantly. "I should land the chopper, darlin'."

"Huh?" she sat back blinking, and pointed at a pine-covered ridge. Breath rasping, blood thumping, she hazily noted Pacer's skillful landing in a glade not far from the rough plank home of Rance Caleb.

Pacer Dillon had just loosened another protective chunk of her being. Should she berate him—or celebrate?

A grizzled man ambled out of the rough shingled cabin. A battered hat on his head, pipe in his mouth, he stared at the new arrivals. A shotgun was cradled in his left arm. His right arm was in a sling.

When Colm started to open the door and jump out, Pacer held her back with an arm around her waist. "I'll go first. He looks loaded for bear."

"Don't be silly. That's Rance."

"I don't give a damn. I'll go first."

Colm had never heard that steel sound in Pacer's voice. Gone was the honey drawl. "But—"

"Shh. Wait one minute." He unfastened the hatch and stepped out, his hands held away from his sides. "I come as a friend, Rance Caleb."

"I dunno ya."

"Uncle Rance, it's me, Colm." Colm almost tumbled in her hurry to get to the two men who were facing each other like pit bulls at the ready.

The pipe drooped, the gun muzzle went down, and a grin split the leathery face like a half-moon. "Colm? Baby? Is it you?"

"Yes. What happened to your arm?" Colm sped past Pacer to Rance's arms. Not that he was able to grip her with the gun and the sling impeding him, but he tried.

Pacer saw the open affection between the two and relaxed, though he continued to study the surrounding rough, dry terrain. "I don't suppose he got it wrestling a steer," he murmured. The older man gave him a narrow-eyed look and Pacer knew he'd caught what he said.

"You got that right," Rance muttered.

"What are you talking about?" Colm pulled back from Rance, her gaze going from him to Pacer.

"It's man talk, darlin'." Pacer grinned when he saw the blood rise in her face. "Did you want to be included?"

"Man's got guts," Rance said, "or he ain't never seen that right cross a yourn." He cackled delightedly when Colm rounded on him, then she kissed his cheek.

"Pacer, this is Rance Caleb. Rance, this is Pacer Creekwood Dillon."

"Indian. Right?"

"Right."

A tiny smile barely cracked Rance's face. "Makin' a run at my little girl, are ya?"

"Yes."

"No," Colm answered at the same time Pacer did.

"Looks like it to me." Rance Caleb's laugh was like dried mesquite rustling out of his throat. Then his smile faded. "You can come in the house and set a spell, but I don't want you to stay here too long. It ain't for you around here anymore, child. You'd better skedaddle and take your friend with ya."

"No. I brought him here for a picnic over by the pond."

"Can't get near the pond anymore. All wired up. Had to get rid a' the last a' my cattle or they'da died a' thirst."

"But—but that water belongs to you just like it does to Boru. You have an agreement with the family, and it's in writing."

"It don't count for much, I can tell ya. I got a lawyer and showed my proof, but they . . ." Rance's voice trailed off, and he looked from Colm to Pacer. "Better to get her outta here."

Colm stared at the old man. "Did they break your arm?"

"Don't s'pose they set out to do it." Rance turned abruptly and went into the house, Colm at his heels.

"Never mind the lemonade, Uncle Rance. You tell me now what happened."

"Tell her," Pacer commanded softly, following them.

"I went up to the pond to cut their damn wire and they caught me and tossed me around some. I called the Texas Rangers, but when they come the wire had an openin' large enough for cattle."

"We'll need aerial shots," Pacer said. "I'll do it now." He left the cabin and strode rapidly toward the helicopter.

"What?" Colm stared out the door after him. "Where are you going? Wait for me." She raced after Pacer, Rance at her heels. "Stop!"

"I'll be back before you can miss me, darlin'. And I have a camera." Pacer revved the engine after he had secured the hatch; then he was airborne almost at once.

"Pacer Creekwood Dillon! Come down here." Colm cupped her hands around her mouth to shout, then let her hands fall. "He could get hurt," she mumbled.

"And it would matter?" Rance asked.

"Yes . . . and I damn well don't know why it should."

"I shoulda had a talk with ya afore now if ya don't know the answer to that."

"Did you know you have a downright dirty laugh?"

"So they tell me. How long ya known this feller?"

"A few days."

"Happens like that sometimes." Rance looked up at the sky, as hard and bright as a blue ceramic plate. "I 'member your ma had a love that come like lightnin'. . . ."

"I'll never see what she saw in my father," Colm said abruptly. "Call me unnatural if you will."

" 'Twarn't your pa. Never knew who it was. Married your pa, but she had a great love that wasn't Vince Collamer."

Colm whirled to face him. "Uncle Rance, why haven't you ever told me this?"

"Never thought much about it. Is it important to ya?"

"Anything I could know about my mother is important to me."

"Shoulda guessed that. She was like my own child, was with me as much as she was with your grandpa."

"Because you and grandpa were always together."

"Yep. Best man ever lived. And your grandma . . . well, she was as tough as old boots but a real lady."

Colm sighed. "I wish I could have known my grandmother or my mother." She scanned the sky. "Do you think he's all right?"

"I think he'd be all right in a cave a' rattlers, Colm

honey. He's tough. More than tough, he's iron, seems like."

Pacer circled the ranch, admiring the expanse. Though he'd left too quickly to get directions, he figured the pond that Colm and Rance had spoken of would border Rance's place, and that it would be large enough to be easily spotted from the air. And so it was.

Angling the helicopter and holding it steady, he took several shots of the area from every angle. There was no opening in the wire surrounding the pond large enough for a person, let alone a small herd.

When the gunfire started, Pacer was caught off guard. Then years of battle training kicked in and he made counter moves to get out of harm's way. The firing continued until he was out of range, two of the shots nicking the helicopter's windshield.

Minutes later he was landing in the glade near Rance's cabin. Colm and Rance were waiting for him.

As he opened the door and jumped out, Colm was on him. "Why did you go without me?" Her arms were around him, her fists pummeling his back.

Rance chuckled. "Stop that, child. You'll cave in the man's spine."

"Not true, sir," Pacer said. "I'm enjoying every touch." When Colm looked up at him, he kissed her hard. "I'm glad you missed me, darlin'."

"Someone shootin' at ya?" Rance pointed with his pipe at the front of the chopper.

"Yeah."

Colm's fists opened and she clutched Pacer's shoulders. "Who did it?"

"Didn't get a look at them."

Pacer heard the sound of a Jeep and instinctively pushed Colm behind him. Almost in the same motion he reached into the cab of the helicopter for any kind of weapon.

The Jeep was coming fast.

Rance wheeled around and hurried toward his cabin.

Colm saw the Jeep break through the trees, saw that a man standing in the front held a gun trained their way.

Pacer let fly with the short-handled crowbar he'd taken from the helicopter. The spiraling missile took the man down like a saber chop.

The gun flew from the Jeep as the vehicle screeched to a halt. The driver reared up, gun in hand.

"Don't try it," Rance said. "I'll kill ya." He stood with the rifle braced on his hurt arm.

"He will too," Colm said quietly. "He can take a fly off a horse's ear with that gun."

The driver dropped his weapon, sparing no glance for his unconscious companion.

"Now, nice and easy," Pacer said, "you get down from there." He approached the man, staying out of Rance's line of fire. "Who sent you?"

The man glared at Pacer, his arms in the air.

"You might have hurt my lady," Pacer told the man gently. "That angers me more than I can say. Now, if I have to ask you again, I'm going to break both your arms."

"You can try." The man crouched and leaped at Pacer in one fast motion.

Pacer was ready. Putting his anger behind it, he brought up his right hand and hit the other man so hard, the attacker's head snapped back, then he dropped to the ground. "Now, do you talk—or do we go around some more?"

"That was some punch," Rance said admiringly.

"Yes." Colm stared at Pacer. Who and what was he? she wondered yet again.

"The owners of Boru don't like trespassers," the man said. "They figured the helicopter might be from here, so they decided to warn off whoever it was." The man rubbed his jaw the whole time he spoke. His words were disjointed, with a great many pauses between them, as though talking was painful.

"And if the helicopter wasn't here," Pacer asked, "were you going to give Rance Caleb another warning?"

"He was told to get off this land," the man said glumly.

"This is Rance's land," Colm said spiritedly.

"Not according to the deed belonging to Mr. Webster."

"Milo Webster is a crook," she burst out. "He stole that property."

Pacer put his arm round her. "Let the man talk, darlin'. Go on."

"Nothing more to say."

"Oh, I think I'd like to know why you shoot at people who fly over the ranch. Talk."

"Ask Mr. Webster—oof."

Pacer hauled the man to his feet and got a strangling grip around his neck. The man struggled to free himself, hoarse sounds issuing from his throat.

"Pacer?" Colm didn't know the savage who was throttling Webster's henchman. "You're killing him."

"Shh, I imagine he knows that," Rance said quietly.

"I don't think he will have much patience with anyone hurting you, my baby."

"Pacer—please."

Pacer turned his head toward Colm. "What?"

"Release him—please."

The man sank to the ground, coughing and choking. When he was able to lift his head, he looked up at Pacer. "I . . . don't . . . know . . . any more."

"He might be tellin' the truth," Rance said, and Pacer turned away from the man on the ground.

"Maybe. And maybe I'd better go over there and ask Mr. Webster what the hell he's doing." Pacer hauled the man to his feet. "Tie him in the shade, Rance. And call the Texas Rangers. I'll be back."

"No!" Colm exclaimed. "I'm going with you. And don't bother shaking your head. You don't know those people. I do."

Pacer hesitated. "I don't want—"

"I'm going." She marched around him to the helicopter and climbed into the passenger seat.

"Let 'er go, boy. She's tough like her ma and grandpa."

"Will you be all right, Rance?"

Rance laughed harshly, his glance sliding from the man he was tying to a tree to the one who was still out cold. "Yep, I'll be fine."

"We won't be long."

"Watch your back. But then I'll bet you learned that killin' way of yourn somewheres. Nam?"

Pacer nodded and strode to the helicopter. Then he hesitated and walked back to Rance, taking a card from his pocket. "Call this number and tell them there's trouble, that I'll be delayed but that I'll call when I can. Thanks."

When they were airborne, Colm turned to him, threading her fingers together. "Milo Webster has been arrested a few times, even indicted, but he's always managed to get away virtually unscathed."

"Wily, is he?"

"Yes."

Pacer looked at her and smiled. "I've been known to be tricky at times myself."

She laughed shakily. "You're not scared, are you?"

"No, but I'm a wary cuss."

"Good." She pointed down. "There. That's the helipad."

As they settled to earth, several gun-toting men appeared from out of the shelter of the trees and waited.

"Let me talk to them first, darlin'."

"All right, but I should identify myself to them."

"Maybe." Pacer stepped from the helicopter and lifted her to the ground. "My name's Pacer Creekwood Dillon. Your boss has been after my company to supply him with heavy equipment."

"We have no orders about arrivals," one man said.

"You shouldn't sell anything to them," Colm muttered.

"I wouldn't," Pacer whispered. "But I remember the name from a request form AbWenDil received."

"You'd be doing business with snakes then."

"It happens." He hadn't looked at her once during the exchange, but watched the men who'd formed a semicircle in front of them.

One of the men walked over to a small metal box affixed to a post and made a call, then approached Pacer. "I want to see identification . . . and the dolly waits here."

"I'm no dolly," Colm said stiffly. "I'm Colm Fitzroy."

Pacer was caught between amusement and wariness when the man whirled to stare at her. "Easy, fella. She's my lady and she goes with me."

"Yeah? Let's see the ID."

Pacer produced his driver's license, as did Colm. Then he stared at the man. "Let's move," Pacer said as the man scrutinized the licenses. "I'm a businessman and I don't stand around and chat."

The man would have said more, but he backed down at Pacer's hard look. "I have to call back and tell them you can go through."

"Then do it."

"Are you trying to antagonize him?" Colm spoke from the side of her mouth.

"Don't twist your lips like that, darlin'. Your mouth's too sweet."

"Mr. Dillon, this way please."

The first man and another armed man led them to a Jeep. The two men got in front, and Pacer and Colm got in the back. The ride was a quick one over rough, dry terrain with rocks abounding everywhere, including in the dirt road.

Pacer looked around him. "Quite a spread."

"Yes," Colm said softly. She pointed to a knoll crowned by a copse of trees. "That's where my tree house was. Uncle Rance built it for me. Maybe it's still there. I never did tell my father where it was."

Pacer took her hand. "Maybe we'll climb up to it together."

She tried to smile, feeling comforted by his touch. "I don't think that will happen." When had they become so close? she wondered. No one had ever felt as comfortable as Pacer Creekwood Dillon, as safe.

"Don't count it out yet, darlin'."

She stared at his profile, but didn't say any more. Though they spoke in low tones, the driver and guard in the front could catch what they were saying.

When she saw the sprawling ranch house, tears welled up in her eyes. Her home! How she'd missed it. She hadn't realized how much until that moment.

Pacer felt the tremor that passed through her and squeezed her hand.

The Jeep screeched to a stop in front of the low porch, throwing up clouds of dust.

"That's Milo Webster," Colm murmured to Pacer, indicating a man standing on the porch between two other men. "I'm not sure about the other two. I think I've seen one of them before, but I'm not sure."

Pacer helped her out of the Jeep, keeping her at his side as he approached the trio.

The man in the middle moved forward, hand outstretched. "I recognize you from your picture in *Forbes* magazine, Mr. Dillon. How are you? I didn't expect a personal answer to my business query."

"I had to be in Houston on business. When Ms. Fitzroy said that she had once owned Boru, I recalled that it was the place on your letterhead."

"Actually her father, my close friend, owned this place and sold it to me."

"Actually," Colm said, "this place was owned by my mother's company, Fitzroy's, and wasn't for sale."

Milo Webster stared at Colm for a moment, then his laughter boomed forth. "Why, little lady, you're as tough as your father was."

"I'm nothing like my father," Colm shot back, making one of the men beside Webster stiffen.

"Uh, these are associates of mine," Webster said. "This is Stefan Denys and this is Claus Berndt. Won't you come in, Ms. Fitzroy, Mr. Dillon?" Webster stood aside and gestured to the door.

Colm opened her mouth to speak, but Pacer squeezed her hand warningly and she was quiet.

Rance had tied up the second man and had been pacing since. Now when he heard the whirr of the helicopter he stalked to the glade, his gun cradled in his left arm.

When the helicopter landed, Colm was the first one out. She ran to him and put her arms around him. Shudders raced through her.

"So, it hurt to see the place."

"Oh yes, it hurt. Manuela cried when she saw me . . . and—and Webster was so brusque with her, so nasty." Colm shook her head.

Pacer approached them, his gaze on Rance. "Can I use your phone?"

"Inside. It's a party line, but I made the call to those people."

Pacer nodded and glanced at Colm. Her face was still at Rance's shoulder, and his mouth tightened.

In the darkened cabin he went to the wall phone and dialed the operator, asking to be put through to New York. "Dev? Uh, I talked to Milo Webster about the heavy equipment. A clean deal, the same as we had in Saigon. Yeah. Oh, that would be good. I look forward to seeing you. Check the invoice to see what's wanted. Very nice place Boru." Pacer replaced the phone slowly.

"What did you really say to your friend?"

He turned and looked at Colm. Her chin was up, there was a raw, hot look in her eyes, but she didn't waver. "I asked for a check on the ranch, the purchase, the taxes, the kind of people who own it."

"Just like that . . . and your friend would know what to do."

"I would say that by now the wheels are in motion. Dev is a devil when he gets going. Nothing stops him. Con is an iron man. You can't take him down easily."

"Sounds like an army."

"It is." He moved closer and took her in his arms, pressing his mouth gently against hers.

She relished the soothing sensation of being held by him, but it was soon replaced by a roaring fire that surged with white heat, taking her away.

"I thought I'd come in outta the sun," Rance said, "but it's hotter in here. I could leave again."

Colm pulled away from Pacer. "No, don't," she said, a little flustered and out of breath.

"Do stay," Pacer drawled.

"Goin' ta draw down on me, young fella?"

"Maybe."

Rance chuckled, striking a wooden match on his overalls. "Yep, reminds me a' Colm, her grandfather, when we were kids." He held the match to his pipe and paused until it was lit. "We went to the same school. I was a small varmint them days, but Colm wouldn't let anybody pick on me. We were more than brothers. I still miss him." Rance puffed on his pipe. "The old man found me in a dry gulch when I was a young un'. Brought me up with Colm. I ran the ranch. Colm went to school. Poor Colm."

Colm laughed out loud. "Mother said you were always needling him about that."

"Yep."

"And that's how you got your name, Caleb?" Pacer asked. "From Colm's great-grandfather?"

"Yep."

Pacer stared at the older man and Rance met his gaze steadily, still puffing on his pipe.

When Colm saw Rance's slow smile, she frowned. "What's up? Why do you look that way, Uncle Rance?"

"Your friend here is not totally sure I've your best interests at heart. Right?"

Colm whirled to face Pacer, catching his slight nod. "But that's ridiculous. Uncle Rance has always supported me on everything."

Pacer shrugged. "Great."

Her chin lifted. "I'd trust Uncle Rance with my life . . . and I've *known* him all my life. Why should I trust you? A man I've known less than forty-eight hours."

"I don't have the answer to that, but I do know that you do trust me."

A tremor shot through her, but she made no response.

"And I trust you," Rance said slowly. "I think she'll need friends down the road."

"So do I."

"Now you're both being cryptic. Explain," Colm said sharply.

"Your uncle and I feel that you will have a tough time handling Fitzroy's, and that you won't be able to get your ranch back without a long, tough legal battle . . . and some fancy footwork."

Pacer's lazy smile seemed to ripple over her like a desert wind, burning and yet soothing, cooling. "And—and you think you can help out with that."

"Yes."

Colm couldn't remember ever feeling such palpable relief, such a sense of letting go, a collapsing of the tensions that had needled her for so long. An inner self told her she was a fool, but the voice wasn't strong enough to dampen the growing enthusiasm, the certainty, the trust in Pacer Creekwood Dillon. "What do we do first?"

Colm's reaction nearly floored Pacer. His heart pounded wildly, and joy was like a river running through him. The need to protect her rose in him like a flood. "First, we find out what's going on with Webster, what it has to do with the ranch . . . and Fitzroy's. Second, we find out how to get that ranch back into your hands. Third, we decide whether it's better for you to have Fitzroy's, or whether I should have it. Don't get starchy, darlin'. If you insist on keeping Fitzroy's that's your business, but for the time being I think it should belong to AbWenDil. If someone's going to get tough, we'll handle it."

Colm gazed at Pacer, then her glance slid to her uncle, who was nodding slowly. "I'll want a paper saying that Fitzroy's is really mine," she said.

"Agreed."

"I don't want anyone fired."

"Fine."

"And . . . I want to be in on what's going down."

"You talk like a cop, darlin'."

She lifted her chin. "Agreed?"

"All right."

Pacer looked at Rance Caleb for a long moment. "If something comes up, don't use the phone, use the radio. I'll give you the frequency we use. Don't take chances. If trouble comes, go to ground, don't face them. Our people can be here in five minutes."

"Sounds even more like a bloody army," Colm muttered.

Pacer grinned. "And I repeat, it is." He turned back to Rance. "If there's trouble brewing, use Colm's name three times in sentences close together. People will show up at your door, all briefed and committed. They will identify themselves by saying Heller sent them. That's the name of my good friend's wife and not a common one. Call on the radio every day, at least twice, at eight and noon or any other time you choose, but don't break the rhythm of two, or an army will descend on you."

"Understood."

As Colm listened to the two men, her mind began to churn. Danger! Pacer felt it and was preparing for it.

When they walked out to the helicopter, Colm kissed Rance several times. "Won't you change your mind and come with us?"

"Nope. This is my land. Takin' care a' Fitzroy land is all I know, child, and I can keep an eye out from here. Somehow, some way, Boru is going to belong to you again. Your great-grandpa, grandpa, and ma wouldda wanted that."

"And they would want you to be safe."

"I know that, and I'll be careful. I don't know how your pa managed to hornswoggle the ranch from your ma, but I can't rest until it's back where it belongs. Caleb and Colm would expect that a' me."

"Be careful."

"Yep."

Once in the air and headed back to Houston, Pacer threaded his fingers through hers. "It's going to be all right."

"But what if they try to hurt him again?"

"That won't happen. People are on the way, very canny street fighters who will protect him. He'll know they're there, but no one else will."

"Street fighters on a ranch that has thousands of acres of wild land? What would they know about handling themselves in such a place?"

"Some of them fought in Vietnam. Others have been mercenaries, fighting in the Middle East and Africa. They're well trained and loyal to the families."

"Meaning you and your associates?"

"Yes."

Colm studied his profile, the hard planed cheek and jawline, the crooked nose, the tight mouth. "You're a tough dude, aren't you?"

He glanced at her. "When I have to be. I'm more inclined to be a lover."

"There was surprise in your voice. Why?"

"Because I just discovered that facet of myself." He smiled at her, watching the color run up in her face.

"Shouldn't you keep your eyes straight ahead?"

"Automatic," he said softly, his gaze roving her face. "You have wonderful skin, so clear and white. You must sunburn."

"I would if I allowed it. I do a great many things in the sun, but I always wear a good sunscreen."

"I'd like to put it on next time, ma'am."

The image in her mind of his strong hands stroking over her naked body had her gasping. "You're a demon, aren't you?"

"I'll be anything you want, ma'am."

Once again he'd thrown her off-balance. "That's Houston up ahead," she said, trying to find her control again.

"Your husky voice deepens when you're excited. That excites me."

"Try cold showers," she said briskly.

"How far does your blush go?"

"Hadn't we better prepare for landing?"

"All right, I'll change the subject. Do you fly?"

"Some, but I'm not sure of myself."

"I'll make a point of tutoring you."

"Thank you."

"That was said very demurely. Changing colors on me?"

"I'm not a chameleon."

"Testy, too."

"Am not." Colm did all she could to stem her smile, but it broke through anyway. Why did Pacer Creekwood Dillon have the power to put her at ease, relax her, give her amusement, a sense of lightness and . . . security?

"You're very beautiful, ma'am."

"Uh, thank you."

"And polite."

"And you're outrageous."

"So I've been told."

"Tell me about those partners of yours."

"What can I say? That Dev and Con searched for

me once, ground-hopping a helicopter through Vietcong territory until they found me? I was wounded, and there wasn't enough room in the chopper, so Con put me in and told Dev to take off. Then he made his way back on his own through some of the most hostile territory in the country."

"You love your friends," she said quietly.

"Very much. They also happen to be married to the two most beautiful women in the world—or so I thought until you came along."

"Thank you."

"I think we'll have beautiful children." He smiled when she gasped.

Four

"I wish Uncle Henry could have come," Colm said as their plane taxied to the terminal at La Guardia Airport. Then she would be staying in a hotel, she added silently, not in Pacer Dillon's home. But he had a housekeeper, she reminded herself, then decided she was being silly. She didn't need a chaperon. Why was she so edgy?

Pacer took her hand. "Henry Troy is a very conscientious executive vice-president. I can see why he'd want to stay if you were leaving."

"I don't know how you talked me into coming to New York."

"I promised you that we would return in a week, that's how."

"Oh." She turned to look at him, smiling. She couldn't remember a time when she had let her guard down so much with anyone. But Pacer had walked into her life and begun smoothing out the ruts almost at once. She frowned, thinking of one major rut in particular.

"What is it?" he asked.

"I was wondering if there was any more news about the Boru."

"I don't think I've ever heard anyone put a 'the' in front of their ranch name as you do from time to time."

"My great-grandfather was Irish. Both his mother and father were from Ireland, and they revered Brian Boru, the legendary Irish hero. It was a habit of his, his son's, and my mother's to refer to the ranch that way."

"Tradition-bound, are you?"

"Aren't you?"

"About some things, maybe. But I think I'm more of a mongrel than you, and we mongrels tend to make our own traditions as we go along."

"What are you besides Creek?"

"A mix of Irish, like you, and Scottish, with a dash of French."

"I heard a bit of tension in your voice. You're not close to your family?"

"I was close to my parents, but they died when I was pretty young. I spent some time in foster homes. Because he'd been a friend of my father's, a local priest tutored me in the classics. Another man who knew my father took me in hand when I was a teenager. Then I went to Princeton."

"On scholarships," Colm murmured. "I read dossiers, too."

"Do you now?"

"You met your friends at Princeton."

"Earlier than that for one of them. And yes, they are my family."

"And I'll be meeting them all this evening?"

"Don't be nervous. They'll love you and you'll feel the same."

Colm nodded, trying to mask her doubts as she gazed at the New York skyline. In less than three hours she would meet the people who loved this man and whom he loved. Why did that shake her so?

The time sped by. A limousine carried them to Pacer's elegant town house on the east side of Manhattan. Because of the heavy traffic they were late arriving. Colm only had time to meet Pacer's housekeeper before she had to begin dressing for dinner.

She was affixing her crystal earrings when she heard a knock on her bedroom door. "Come in," she called, and Pacer opened the door. "What is it?" she asked. "Am I late?"

"No. I missed you." He quickly crossed the room and took her in his arms, kissing her gently, urging her lips to part.

His hands floated down her body, skimming the curves, pausing at the intriguing indentations. His breathing was short and rough, and his blood thundered in his ears. "You're magic to me, Colm Fitzroy," he whispered. Shock held him immobile as the word love rose in his mind, a word he'd been sure he would never use with a woman again. Yet it was there now in the front of his mind. Colm had moved into him and taken him. How? When?

His words swept over Colm like a soft breeze. Forcing her eyes open, she looked up at him. "Magic is for children."

"Is it?" A finger stroked her cheek. "Your skin feels like velvet."

"You move too fast, Dillon." Nettles of doubt made her pull back. She trusted Pacer. Could she trust her own responses? She was catapulting into—what? Love? That could be a twisted thing. Did she trust the word? She trusted the man.

"I can get from A to B," he said, staring into her eyes. "With you I can get there much faster."

His calm voice, the implication of a commitment, shattered her. Tremors tore through her body. "I have to be free."

"Be free to do anything but leave me, Colm. Yet even if you leave me I'll still be with you. Sometimes it's like that."

What had Rance said about her mother having a lightning love? She eyed him warily. "We don't know each other."

"What's to know? Ask me anything, I'll tell you." The last of his fences fell and trust spilled into his being. If he'd known at that moment he'd be beheaded for telling her his name, he would have shouted it from the rooftops. Colm had changed his life, filled the dark corners of his heart with light, colored his existence with the entire spectrum.

"Shouldn't we be going?" she asked, turning away.

"Yes." He took her arm and led her to the door.

"Are you going to talk to him tonight, Con?" Dev asked.

"Yes. He was more cryptic than usual on the phone this morning, but I got the feeling that Colm Fitzroy is in danger and he was afraid to come to New York without her."

"Afraid? Pacer?" Dev's eyebrows rose to black points.

"I know. I reacted the same way when he used the word." Con shook his head as he poured himself some seltzer water. "That's what keyed me to the trouble. That phone call was pretty obscure, but there was a great deal of tension in his voice. I hadn't heard that since . . ."

"Da Nang," Dev said flatly. "Then I guess we'd better talk to him this evening."

Con nodded, frowning.

Colm stepped from the limousine and looked up at the Manhattan high rise. Why should she be nervous? she asked herself, and took a deep breath. It was silly.

"They'll love you, darlin'."

"Stop reading my mind."

"You get testy when you feel threatened." He kissed her hair, his fingers caressing her neck.

"Pacer . . ." Her voice was thready and uneven as she resisted the urge to sink into his embrace. When had he stepped up the courtship to warp speed? She had thought she was in for a slow sweet interlude. Now she felt as though she were on a fast ride down a velvet mountain with no handholds or steering. "Don't press me."

Though her voice was soft, Pacer heard the lacing of panic. Something or someone had frightened her. He touched a finger to her lips. "You call the shots.

As long as you don't push me out of your life, I'll do what you ask."

His gentle voice and tender words pierced her. "Would you go to hell if I requested it?"

"Probably not."

"Then I'll save my breath." She couldn't quite control the shiver of delight that coursed through her when he kissed her again.

"It's too warm a night for you to be cold," he whispered against her neck.

"We're gathering a crowd." She pushed back from him, looking away from those sharp eyes, then walked unsteadily toward the entrance to the high rise.

In the elevator, Pacer leaned down and kissed her chin. "May I kiss your mouth?"

"It's a little late to ask," she said acerbically, wishing she could control the smile that was forcing its way to her lips.

"Thank you." He scooped her into his arms and took her mouth, his lips pressing insistently against hers, forcing them to part. Tongue to tongue they clung.

The kiss went on endlessly. Colm could feel her body and mind fragment and join with his. Groaning, she twined her arms around his neck, her body molding tight to his.

The elevator doors opened, exposing the passionately embracing couple to the people waiting in the foyer for them.

Dev put his arm around his wife, his fingers massaging her distended abdomen. "Felicity, darling, let's go home."

"Stop, beast," she told him lovingly, leaning against him as she always did. "You're still bad in an elevator."

"You told me I was good."

"Shh."

Con Wendel hugged his own wife. "Love, let's send these people home."

"Con, stop. Isn't she pretty? Those long legs and slender body. Umm, I think he picked a winner."

"Like you." Con kissed her neck.

"I'm delighted," Con's father said. "It's time he settled down."

"We should have the wedding reception for them, dear, don't you think?" Con's mother asked sunnily.

The older man smiled down at her. "Pacer will let us know about that."

The conversation penetrated fuzzily into Colm's consciousness. Opening one eye, she saw the people in her peripheral vision. They were smiling and watching! "Oh!" Pushing back from Pacer, Colm stared at the six strangers in growing alarm.

Pacer reluctantly dropped his hands from her body and smiled at his friends. "Con, that elevator moves too damned fast."

"Sorry about that." Con grinned.

"How do you do, Ms. Fitzroy?" Heller said, stepping forward. "I'm Heller Wendel and this is my mother-in-law and father-in-law . . ." Her manner serene, Heller quickly introduced everyone.

Colm politely greeted all of them, knowing there wasn't a snowball's chance in hell that she'd remember anyone's name. She wasn't sure she knew her own. She did notice that Pacer's friends were all attractive. Heller Wendel was a tall blond amazon, Felicity Abrams a stunning beauty with raven-dark hair and alabaster skin. The two men would turn women's heads wherever they went, Con with his

athletic body and handsome face; Dev with his chis-
eled features and compelling blue eyes.

Pacer put his arm around Colm, drawing her close
to his side. "Isn't she a beauty, Heller?"

"Yes, she is." Heller smiled at Pacer and kissed
Colm on the cheek. "You are most welcome to our
home."

Colm had been prepared to be uncomfortable, but
the enthusiasm and warmth of Pacer's friends charmed
her totally.

"And these are our children," Heller went on, indicating a dark-skinned teenage boy and two younger
children, "and these two are Dev's and Felicity's
youngsters."

Colm forgot everything as the enchanting children
surrounded her, all talking at once.

"Do you think she'll survive our active progeny?"
Con asked Pacer.

Pacer stared steely-eyed at Con, his mouth hardening. "I wish that was all that worried me."

"Let's go to the study," Dev said. He looked at his
wife and nodded his head slightly.

"Why don't we take Colm with us upstairs?" Felicity suggested, gathering the children and smiling at
Colm. "Maybe that will help settle down the group."

Colm felt a shiver of fear when she glanced at
Pacer and saw how grim-faced he and his friends
were. "Pacer?"

"I'll be right in the study, darlin'."

"All right." A coldness seemed to settle in her heart
as he turned and walked down a wide hall with the
other men. It was as though a part of her had been
sheared off. The pain was sharp, the loss keen, and

her old fear of giving up control to another rose within her. Not all of Pacer's warmth kept it at bay.

Pacer said nothing even after the study door was closed and he was alone with his two closest friends.

"Talk, Pace," Dev said. "We got the message that you wanted some ferreting done."

"You're right, Dev—but I want more than that."

"You didn't come east alone, and we assume you're worried about the lady."

Pacer's smile was hard. "You got it first time. I brought Colm up here because I had a feeling she was in imminent danger."

"Imminent? How so?" Dev sat down in a leather chair, stretching his long legs out in front of him.

"I'll bet it's not that tangible," Con said. "Got a bad feeling?"

Pacer nodded. "On the ranch. I met Milo Webster. the man gives off powerful vibes."

"Negative ones," Dev murmured.

"What did you find out?" Pacer asked.

Dev pointed to a bound notebook on the desk.

Con picked it up and opened it, flipping through the pages. "He's wealthy, new money, say in the last ten years—What is it?"

"Colm's father became partners with Webster about four or five years ago," Pacer said slowly. "The partnership with Vince Collamer ended when Collamer's car went out of control and hit a tree several months ago. Now Colm is in charge of Fitzroy's and, I would assume, Vince Collamer's estate."

"You're thinking your lady has been scammed, and maybe could be at risk," Con said.

Pacer's smile was crooked. "In her mind she isn't my lady yet, Rad."

"But you know it, even if she never accepts it," Dev said dryly. "I know all about that."

"Yeah, I guess you do." Pacer's smile faded. "What do I do? She won't stay here very long. She's committed as hell to Fitzroy's and its employees, plus the future of the people Collamer fired from the firm in the last couple of years."

Con picked up some other papers. "Colm's been busy. She's made some drastic changes in the place and the curve is up, but she wouldn't be able to fight a hostile takeover. Her liquid assets are marginal."

"So we carry her," Pacer said firmly, eyeing the other two.

"We could take a whopping loss," Con said easily.

Dev grinned. "Down for the count, maybe."

"But we're doing it," Pacer said tightly, and he relaxed when the other two nodded.

"Risk-taking is one of our strong points," Dev said lazily.

Colm was entranced with the children, and Felicity, Heller, and Con's parents helped to put her at ease. She laughed and chatted with the other adults and played with the children, feeling herself unwind more and more. she hadn't been so comfortable with strangers for years. She was kneeling on the floor admiring a drawing by the youngest Abrams child when a kiss feathered her neck.

She jumped and turned to see Pacer smiling at her. "Oh. Hi."

"Hi yourself." He leaned down and picked her up, holding her against him, her feet inches above the floor. "I missed you," he said and fixed his mouth to hers.

The children's giggling didn't penetrate the sensual haze that Pacer's kiss wove around Colm, but she did hear the shushing of the parents. Pulling back with an effort, she tried to free herself. "Stop, Pacer."

"No. Kids, cut it out. Don't laugh at your uncle," he said, and kissed her again. "See? Now it's fine."

"You're outrageous," she said breathlessly.

"Are you going to carry her downstairs?" one of the children asked.

"Should I?"

"Yes, Uncle Pacer, do it," they chorused.

"Stop that," Felicity said to the children, though she couldn't quite mask her smile. "Now behave. You can play games for another hour, then Nanny will put you to bed."

The children immediately began grousing about that. Pacer set Colm down and she managed to say good night to the children.

"I don't need a nanny," Simeon, the oldest child, Heller and Conrad's adopted son, said.

"I'm sure you don't." Colm shook his hand solemnly.

Out in the upstairs hall, Pacer looked at her. "So Simeon wove his magic around you as well."

"Yes. Is he your favorite?"

"I love them all, but he is pretty special to Dev and me. He was the first child, and he's very unusual. And smart." Pacer smiled. "He wants to go to Princeton."

"And follow in your footsteps . . ."

"And his father's and Dev's." He put his arm around her and led her down the stairs.

Dinner was fun. Colm relaxed, laughed, and had a good time. She was sorry the senior Wendels couldn't stay, but they had a previous engagement. She was also impressed with Conrad Wendel and Deveril Abrams, and was amazed at the rapport among the three men. Time and again, one would begin a sentence and another would finish it.

Had there ever been such laughter in her life? she wondered. She felt so warm. Each time she looked at Pacer, the heat rose in her. He gave her not just sensual glances, but caring ones as well. Despite the warning bells going off inside her, a change was taking place. Pacer was weaving a gossamer cocoon around her. Struggling out of it would be foolish. All her life she'd battled to be her own person, never to become the victim of any man. Keeping men at arm's length had done that. Now this impossible man was twining around her, warming her, wanting her.

Then she caught a look that passed between Pacer and Con, and her blood congealed. Fear, her ever present companion, reared like a mustang in her mind.

"What's going on?" she asked abruptly. The question was like a bomb in the midst of the lighthearted conversation.

Pacer didn't pretend to misunderstand her. "It's all right, darlin'. I'll tell you everything."

"Everything?"

"Yes."

The simple affirmative soothed her as no flowery phrases could have. She inhaled deeply. "You feel something is wrong with my company, don't you?"

"Not exactly, darlin'. We feel something is wrong with the people around you."

She stiffened. "Who? Not Rance or Uncle Henry."

"Not them." Pacer sipped his after-dinner brandy. "We think that the sale of your ranch to Milo Webster might not have been . . . kosher."

"I told you that," she said bitterly.

Heller and Felicity leaned forward, mouths opened to speak.

"Hold it, you two," Pacer said affectionately. "You'll hear everything too. We couldn't keep anything from you."

"As long as you realize that," Heller muttered, earning a blown kiss from her husband.

"We're tough, too, you know," Felicity added, smiling when her husband winked at her.

"I know that," Pacer said. He sat back in his chair, swirling his cognac around in the glass. "We're running checks on Milo Webster."

Colm laughed sharply. "Don't bother. I tried that. He checks out like Snow White."

Dev chuckled. "But you haven't had Pacer Dillon's friends check him out, Colm. Pacer has friends that even Con and I don't know."

"That's right," Con said. "Pacer does have sources that would make the CIA cringe."

"Who are these people?"

Pacer shrugged. "Friends. Some I met in Nam, some I met here."

"And you trust them?"

"Yes."

Colm nodded. "Then I do too."

A concerted sigh seemed to wing around the table. The smiles were tremulous, but strengthened quickly.

Then Pacer laughed and they all gaped at him.

"He chuckles, but I've never heard him actually laugh before," Heller said wonderingly.

"Not once until now," Felicity said, her voice filled with curiosity. Her gaze swung to Colm then to her husband, who again winked at her.

Colm looked around the table at Pacer's amazed friends, then turned to him. "Everyone here seems not to have heard you laugh. But you laughed the evening you held my dress together. . . ."

"He what?" Dev sat forward in his chair. "Tell all."

"None of your business," Pacer said mildly.

"You can't leave us hanging, Pace, my man," Con said, his face alight with mirth. "You've seen us cave in and surrender. It shouldn't bother you to let us witness your . . . demise."

Colm studied the two couples. "So what you're saying is that he's seen the two of you fall on your faces, and now you want to know if he did?"

"Something akin to that," Dev drawled, chuckling.

"Actually, he didn't fall on his face." Colm smiled at them, then gazed at Pacer, her smile deepening.

"No?" Dev caught her look and glanced at Con, who nodded slowly as though the two of them had just come to a mutual decision. "Explain, then."

"Dev," Pacer said warningly.

"I know. You're going to kill me. I'll have to chance it."

"He won't kill you," Colm said uncertainly when the others nodded. "Well, let me explain."

"Please do." Con kept his gaze on Pacer. "You have a punishing right, friend, but I can't resist."

"I don't pretend to understand all the innuendos," Colm said, "so I'll ignore them. I had a cocktail party at my apartment a few nights ago. I often do. Pacer came. The zipper on the back of my dress split. Pacer stepped behind me and held the dress together. I would have looked a little bare if he hadn't. You see?"

"I'm beginning to," Con murmured, shrugging when Pacer's head whipped his way. "Sorry."

"He helped me toward my bedroom and—well, that part isn't important."

'I've a feeling it's the nucleus," Dev muttered, wincing when his wife pinched him. His smile didn't change when Pacer's look fixed on him. "I think it's going to be a double murder, Con."

"Right."

"Stop it right now," Heller said, glaring at her husband and Dev.

The two men subsided at once.

Pacer unrolled his body from the chair, his hand stretching out to Colm. "Time to go."

She rose to her feet, her head cocked to one side. "Really? Or are you irritated that I told them about the dress?"

"Yes to both."

"Oh." Colm made her good-byes, quite sure she dented good etiquette by her offhandedness, but her head was whirling with the evening, with Pacer Dillon and his friends.

The four looked at each other for long moments after Colm and Pacer left.

"He's mad about her," Felicity said softly. "I think I'm a little jealous. He's belonged to us for so long." She smiled ruefully at Heller.

"She's the most sophisticated innocent I've ever seen," Heller said. "With a touch of pathos."

The two men looked thoughtful.

Felicity caught the vibrations between them. "You're not going to tell us any more, are you?"

"Not right away, darling."

"Soon we'll know more, Heller."

"You haven't said a word since we left your friends," Colm said as Pacer helped her from the limousine. "What is it?"

"I want to love you. What do you want?"

"Uh . . ." She stared up at him as he unlocked the door to his town house. "I want you to at least change expression when you invite me into your bed."

He smiled down at her. "If my features mirrored my thoughts, you might run screaming into the night."

Colm blinked and walked ahead of him into the house. In the kitchen, she turned to face him as he switched on the light. "You want to go to bed with me."

"I want to marry you—tonight. But I promised no pressure, and there won't be any. Close your mouth, darlin', you'll catch flies."

"People . . . don't . . . marry like that."

"Is that a no?"

"We don't know each other."

"I know enough. What bothers you?" He walked past her to the refrigerator and brought out a bottle of Saratoga water and a fresh lime. He poured the mineral water into two glasses and squeezed lime into them. "Got time to discuss it?" He handed her a glass.

She hesitated, wondering where to start. "I don't know how you feel about things."

"I want to marry you . . . forever. Everything else should fall into place nicely."

"Just like that."

"Takes hard work every day and loving all the time."

"You're not a marriage counselor," she said, and gulped her drink. The snap of lime caught in her throat and made her cough.

"No, I'm not a marriage counselor," he said. "You might have to trust me on a few things."

"And do you trust me?"

He nodded slowly and guided her from the kitchen to the sitting room. "From your eyebrows to your ankles, my love, you're the one I believe in, and have from the beginning."

"Oh." She faced him, clutching her glass. "I—I don't—haven't planned on marriage." Perhaps a liaison of sorts some day, she'd thought. Maybe even children, provided she could give them security and love, not the loneliness she'd known. What would Pacer Dillon's children look like? Tall, steely eyed, sturdy. The girls would have blue eyes and his wonderful streaked hair. Sadness settled over her like a cloak. It couldn't be with her. There were too many barriers. She'd spent a lifetime building them.

"I hadn't planned on marriage either," he said. Marriage to Marya had seemed enough. Now he knew that he hadn't even scratched the surface of passionate love. He itched to do that.

"What if we don't suit?" she asked. Just the thought of losing him was painful. She hadn't figured on there being a Pacer Dillon in her life.

"We do." He knew all he needed to know about Colm, but he had to have more of her, peel back to the hidden core, love her dark side, protect her innocence even if she never wanted him.

She looked away from him, her gaze going around the high-ceilinged room as though inspiration would come from the wainscoted walls or French cloth wallpaper. "Chancy."

"Yes." Without her, life would be a string of lusterless gray days.

She turned back to him, her face tight as though her head had begun to ache. "What if—there are many places where a man and woman . . . so many things need to be considered."

Pacer set down his glass and approached her. Again he lifted her in his arms so that their mouths were centimeters apart. "Then explore, delve, research, do your damnedest, but—"

Before he could finish, Colm reached up and placed her lips on his.

He didn't kiss her back, but his tongue came out and laved her lips gently.

Colm let her tongue explore his mouth. When his hands tightened at her waist, bringing her closer to him, she felt his fully aroused body at once. "Pacer. I—I like this." But the specter from long ago hadn't faded altogether.

"Yes." He pulled back, his smile twisted. "As you can see, I respond to you."

"Yes," she said breathily. She was leaning up to kiss him again when she saw a movement out of the corner of her eye. "Oh."

Pacer shot a quick look at Megan, his Irish wolfhound, then his gaze sharpened on Colm. "Frightened of dogs?"

"Noooo . . . but that's not a dog. It's a—a giant."

"Were you ever bitten?"

"Dragged by the arm by one of my father's deerhounds," she said colorlessly. "Barely broke the skin." Still, she'd been terrified out of her head and had screamed for her father. Finally one of the ranch hands had pulled the dog from her. Bruises of the mind stayed longer than those of the body. She could still recall her father berating the man who'd handled his dog too roughly, according to him.

"I see," Pacer said. "Tell Megan to leave then."

"Leave," Colm whispered.

The large canine studied her for a moment, glanced at her master, and about-faced.

Colm exhaled, then looked up at Pacer. He hadn't told her she was silly, nor had he invited her to pet the monster. "Thank you. Where were we?"

He touched her cheek where a blush tinted it red. "There's no need for embarrassment between us, is there?"

"No." The word was barely audible.

"Kiss me, darlin'."

It both titillated and surprised Colm that she had to stand on tiptoe to do it. As tall as she was, without Pacer stooping it would have been impossible for her to reach him. What shocked her was his openmouthed acceptance of her kiss, the taking of her with tongue and lips that was more intimate than anything she'd ever experienced. If his hands hadn't grasped her waist, she might have been too weak to stand.

Slanting his mouth across hers, he lifted her so

that their mouths fit and locked to each other. His tongue plundered her in gentle abandon.

Colm felt fastened to him, but she instinctively knew that if she pulled back, she would be free of him at once. She was his prisoner, yet he set her free. When she felt his hand at the zipper on the back of her dress, she pushed her hair to one side to help him.

The dress didn't drop from her body. It slithered downward, revealing her lace-covered breasts, then stopped at her hips.

She caught the hot look in his eyes and hesitated. Memory was pain. She wouldn't think of that. She undulated her hips until the silken fabric slid to the floor, pooling at her feet. "Feels cool," she murmured. Pleased as she was by the desire in his expression, she couldn't stem the fear that crawled through her. Fragmented pictures of Petey Kelso clicked through her mind.

"It feels hot to me," he said.

She lifted her hands and unbuttoned his shirt, pushing it aside. "I forgot to ask permission," she murmured. A faint panic flushed her body, and moisture coated her skin.

"Feel free, make free. I'm yours."

His smile was like a caress. "Sounds like I own you," she said low and soft.

"Did anyone ever tell you that that hoarseness in your voice is very sexy?"

"No." How could anyone have said that? Pacer was the first man to ever make it happen.

"It is, and yes, you do."

"Do what?" She felt dizzy from looking into his eyes.

"You own me."

"Oh."

He leaned down, his lips touching her eyes, closing them. "Please continue to make free with me."

"In the sitting room?" she asked faintly, her body tingling from scalp to toes.

"At the corner of Fifth and Forty-fifth if you choose."

"This is better."

"Yes." She couldn't quite hide her trepidation, her shaking hands. She knew he wanted her, and hoped he would ignore her obvious nervousness.

In tense concentration she removed his shirt, then her hands hovered over his zipper. No way could she touch him.

"Don't be afraid, darlin'."

"Don't want to catch anything that might pop out." At his rumble of laughter she realized she'd spoken out loud and ducked her head in embarrassment. "My wayward tongue."

"I love your tongue. If you washed my body with it, I'd die a happy man. Blushing again?" He frowned as he gazed down at her. What had caused the sheen of fear on her body, the slight tremor in her hands?

"For a man with the reputation of being reserved, you can certainly speak plain."

"No need to hide our feelings from each other." He caught her chin in one hand and lifted her head. "Are you a virgin, Colm?"

"Technically."

He watched a hardness cloud her eyes. Her whole being seemed to retreat from him.

"Were you raped?"

"You're blunt, Pacer Creekwood Dillon."

"Yes."

"Uncle Henry intervened before the actual penetration. He shot and wounded the man. When he recovered he was put in prison. My father hated my uncle for making a ruckus. He said it blew the incident out of all proportion and that it would damage me." she shook her head. "I was glad my uncle shot him. I wanted him dead."

"Me too." He pulled her close and held her gently, his hands massaging her back. "Did you get therapy?"

"Yes, my uncle insisted on it. My father had never been my friend, but after that there wasn't even an appearance of closeness. I tried to be in his company as little as possible."

Pacer pressed his mouth to her hair. "And the man is still in prison?"

"I think so. The police had been looking for him in connection with other crimes, and he was given a long sentence."

"What's his name?"

"Petey Kelso. why?"

"Just a name for my files, darlin'."

They held each other for a long time, not speaking, as Colm's memories of the horrible attack faded once more. Slowly she became aware of Pacer's strong arms around her, his heart beating steadily beneath her cheek, the heat of their nearly naked bodies pressed close. Desire began to churn within her again, and she shifted restlessly, rubbing her hips against his.

"Where were we?" she asked huskily. She was surprised that the passion was building inside her. She hadn't expected that.

"We were getting ready for bed," he said, telling himself to release her. As much as he wanted her, there was no way he was going to frighten her by demanding too much too soon.

"No, we were getting ready to make love. I want that." She gazed up at him steadily.

He shook his head.

"You told me you were mine," she said.

"So I am."

For the first time Colm saw uncertainty on Pacer's strong features. It made her heart flutter that such a man could be so concerned about her. "I liked what we were doing."

"So did I."

"I was doing pretty well then?" Her better sense was shouting warnings at her, reminding her of all those years of keeping men at bay, adroitly avoiding intimacy. By inviting a man into her life, she could lose the spiritual and mental autonomy she'd fought so hard to get and keep. Was she masochistic?

"Not bad for a beginner," he said.

"Now you're the one whose voice is hoarse."

"Darlin', I'm on fire for you." He gazed intently at her. Her smile didn't quite mask the deep-rooted fear. She'd been badly hurt and frightened, and therapy hadn't erased it all. "But if we're going to wander around Manhattan tomorrow, we should get some sleep."

Disappointment and relief warred in her. She wanted him and feared the intimacy.

Pacer inhaled deeply. Then he bent and swung her up in his arms. "I want you to be happy and unafraid." He kissed her deeply.

"When we do decide to make love, darlin', there'll be no chains on you. You will always have time to back out, my Colm, I promise you that."

"Is that why you're talking through your teeth?"

"I didn't say it would be easy." He carried her out to the hall and mounted the stairs two at a time.

"You're very strong," she said musingly, her arms tightening around his neck. "I don't think I'd like to be your enemy." Was he taking her to bed now, she wondered, despite what he'd said? Excitement and desire overflowed within her.

"No fear of your being my enemy," he said, "even if you stabbed me a thousand times."

"Wouldn't that kill you?" she whispered in his ear.

"That would happen only if you left me."

The blatant confession of need shook her as nothing ever had. His power was elemental, as was his gentleness. Pacer was Zeus—and a lovable puppy. Would she ever know him? Did it matter? "Are we going to your room?"

"No, to yours. You need your sleep."

Despite her spunkiness, Pacer knew there was a wound, an unhealed hurt that she had tried to bury. Some day she might trust him enough to unearth it with him. In the meantime he would protect her from all hurt, from anyone who could damage her, even if it was himself.

His body pulsed with the need to have her, to pleasure her, to give her all things sensuous and loving, and all of him. Never had he wanted to open the secret door inside himself. Not even Marya had known him completely, and he had loved her. With Colm it was more than emotion, it was parts of himself he wanted to present her with. His mind, spirit—all wrapped in ribbons and given to her.

It jarred him to want to open himself to her, be vulnerable to hurt. But he couldn't call back the rush of giving and loving that had erupted in him at the first sight of her. He would die loving her, and he wouldn't change that for anything.

"What are you thinking?" she asked as he reached the top of the stairs.

"That you have me where you want me."

Colm shook her head. It seemed as though he had her. She was getting a little jittery. Her body had cooled down . . . inside and out.

He laid her gently on her bed. "I'll be down the hall if you need me, darlin'."

"Kiss me, Pacer. Take the fear away." She hadn't meant to say that, to expose her deep-seated fright.

"I will, my Colm, I will." Slowly, sweetly, he bent down to her, his hands stroking her as he kissed her. He stretched his long body next to hers on the satin-covered bed. Then his lips slid down her body, kissing her, blowing gently against her bare skin, delighting when she sighed and wriggled closer to him. His desire threatened to overwhelm him. Pulling back, he lifted his head. "I thought I could just kiss you good night and tuck you in. I can't." He kissed her once more, then rolled off the bed to his feet.

Reading the bewilderment and disappointment in her eyes, he almost joined her on the bed again. Swallowing hard, he backed away. "See you in the morning."

Colm stayed where she was, sprawled on the bed,

watching him stride across the bedroom and out the door. Sitting up slowly, she looked around the quiet room. Bereft, cold, and unsatisfied, she fought the ambivalent feelings coursing through her.

Sleep didn't come. Colm tossed and turned. Twice she got up and went to the bathroom. Once she opened her door and glanced down the hall. For two pins she'd go down to Pacer's room and pour cold water on him! No, that wouldn't be the reason she'd go. She wanted him to hold her, keep her close to him. Despite her fear she needed him!

Finally as the Manhattan night was turning gray, she closed her eyes. She dreamed of Boru . . . with Pacer there with her . . . and another specter that dogged them and made her want to scream. Only Pacer kept the banshee at bay, only he kept the fear away.

Five

Colm opened her eyes and knew she wasn't in her own home. Her body was curled up in the middle of the bed. She'd dreamed she was with Pacer. He should have been lying there beside her. Memories of the night rushed over her like a flood. Had she really only dreamed their lovemaking? It had been so real, having him touch her, touching him back.

She sat bolt upright in bed. Could it have been real? Loving Pacer had seemed so natural. She hadn't been able to get enough of him. She had wanted more, more, and they had loved all night. Each time it had been impossibly better. Was Pacer magic? Why hadn't she been afraid of him even with the specter between them?

Staring at the pillow next to hers, she didn't hear the door open.

"You all right, darlin'?"

His voice rumbled across the room, lifting the hairs on the back of her neck. She turned toward the door.

Colm's shy but beaming smile almost made Pacer forget his vow to give her time. The tray of coffee and toast nearly slid from his grasp. He took a deep breath, then grinned at her, his gaze going over her. "I thought we could have coffee together," he said.

"You don't have a meeting this morning?"

"Only with you." He walked over to the bed, settling the breakfast tray on her lap.

Colm swallowed hard as she gazed up at him. He looked good enough covered from chin to ankle. Wearing only a short robe, he was devastating, dangerous as hell. "Thank you for the coffee," she said. "I could have come downstairs."

"Indulge me. You're blushing, darlin'." He pushed aside the covers and sat beside her.

"Why wouldn't I blush? Everything you say is sexy. That is, it has sexual overtones. . . . You know what I mean." Why was she babbling?

He chuckled. "I'm not sure. Shall I leave?"

"Yes—no. Have some coffee." When he moved closer to her, her body flushed as though she'd just been dropped into a hot tub. "Toast?" she asked as she spread jam on her slice.

"Will you put jam on mine too?"

She struggled to keep her hand steady, but a dollop of the strawberry preserve dropped onto her nightgown.

"Let me, please." He leaned over and licked up the bit of jam. "Very good. I'd like more. Strawberry's my favorite." He grinned.

"You're doing that on purpose." Glaring at him did not good, she thought with frustration. He still overflowed with sexuality. He was a damned menace.

"Finish your toast and coffee," he said. "I'm touring Manhattan with you. And we're going to include a visit to Rumpelmayer's on that list."

Colm forgot her anxieties for a moment. "I've been there. When we stayed at the Plaza we—but you guessed that, didn't you?"

He nodded, smoothing her tousled hair back from her face. "It scares me when I think how I argued with Con and Dev about going to Houston, how close I came to not going. It might have taken months for me to have found you."

Colm felt hot and cold all at once, soaring but chained, wild but caged. "We might never have met."

He shook his head. "You are my karma. We had to meet."

Avoiding his eyes she stared at his chest, the arrowing of his hair there. "I thought Indians didn't have body hair." Why had she said that? Now she couldn't keep her eyes off him.

"Maybe some don't. Remember, my father was Irish."

"Will you tell me more about your family someday?"

"Yes." His nostrils flared. "You smell so good."

"Thank you." Melting, that's what she was doing. Be strong, she told herself.

He leaned over and kissed her gently, just above her cleavage. "I thought there was more jam there," he said as he felt her stiffen. "Did I hurt you?"

Yes! Yes, he hurt her. He was knocking down all her defenses. "Maybe we should get dressed."

"Tell me more about the man who attacked you."

That jolted her. "Where did that question come from?" He couldn't know that Petey Kelso dogged her dreams. Nobody knew that.

"You need to talk about it, darlin'." Pacer kissed

her nose. "You said that you weren't raped, but you were scarred." He felt her flinch and his whole body tensed. "Tell me." His hoarse voice was the only outward sign of his agitation, yet his anger was palpable.

"All during the time I was in therapy my father made it plain that he blamed me for what had happened, that I had caused it."

Pacer lifted her, settling her on his lap. "Very archaic attitude and damned unpaternal. It would seem he needed therapy too. Go on, darlin'."

"That's all. I've had nightmares . . . and I still see my therapist from time to time."

Pacer gently touched her face. "To me you're the purest of the pure, undefiled, and when we get out of this bed . . ." He smiled at her angry look. "Well, we are in bed together."

"Only in the most literal sense," she told him tartly.

He stroked her cheek. "You're a brave lady."

His soft voice seemed to peel back the painful scab that had held in the horror for all these years, had allowed it to turn blacker and blacker, get bigger and bigger. Now it spilled from the dark corners of her mind, melting, falling away. Words tumbled from her. "I was afraid of being close to people for a time, even though the therapist told me over and over it hadn't been my fault. And I believed her, despite what my father said. But there were still nightmares."

His arms tightened around her. "All children should be protected from vermin like that."

She lifted her head and stared at him. "I used to think that I wouldn't ever have children, that the world was too dangerous, but I don't have those fears any more." There were other ones, though, deep-seated, hidden fears that she couldn't even describe, the unknown specters that haunted her. Not even to Pacer could she describe the indescribable.

He brushed silky tendrils back from her face. "Colm?"

She inhaled, pushing the black thoughts away. "Children are a big commitment."

"Yes. I watch my friends with theirs. Very intense."

Having Pacer's baby seemed wonderful all at once. Colm stifled the sensation.

Pacer could feel the wariness between them. Colm Fitzroy was a complex person with many layers. He longed to know every one. He touched her shoulder with one finger. "Beautiful."

Delight spun through her. What sort of magic did he have that such a simple touch could make her ache for him?

"Your eyes are widening," he murmured. "Those beautiful jewels are fire and ice."

She looked away, trying to control her desire. "You—you loved your wife, didn't you?"

"Yes."

His answer was expected. What was unexpected was the pain that stabbed through her.

"I met Marya when I was recovering from a wound in a hospital in Saigon. When I was on my feet again, we started the hospital and orphanage for children. And we married. After she was killed I stayed in Nam and got the hospital going again. I still keep in touch with the doctors there."

"And you still love her."

"Yes . . . but I came to terms with losing her." He looked down at Colm. As much as he'd loved Marya, he'd never once experienced the almighty power and need and desire that had assailed him when he'd first seen Colm Fitzroy.

He suddenly lifted her off his lap and rolled off the bed. "Time to see Manhattan," he said, grabbing the tray and nearly sprinting for the door. "We're meeting with Con and Dev at eleven-thirty, but it should be a short meeting."

The door closed behind him, and once more Colm lay sprawled on the bed, blood pressure up, breathing hard. Pacer Dillon was killing her.

After a shower and shampoo she felt better. Dressed in comfortable skirt and blouse and walking shoes, she left her room, armed against Pacer Creekwood Dillon. He was potent, but she could control him.

"Hi," he said as she entered the sitting room, his gaze running hotly over her. "Taxi's waiting."

Manhattan was a jewel. Summer was waning but there was a warm breeze, and fluffy clouds drifted across the soft blue sky. The granite, steel, and glass buildings glittered like polished swords stuck into the earth. The cacophony of traffic, people, whistles, screeches, and horns was wild background music to the world's most exciting city.

When they reached Park Avenue, Colm stopped and looked around her. "It pulses like a heartbeat."

"Yes." Pacer wasn't seeing anything of the city at all. His eyes were fixed on Colm. For these couple of hours they would explore Manhattan, lose themselves in the anonymity of the city, be alone.

Colm was delighted with their outing. Being comfortable with Pacer was something that surprised her. So many times he threw her off stride. But then there were other times. Like now, holding his hand, ambling up and down the streets and avenues. "It is absolutely beautiful. Park Avenue is all I remembered and more."

"Now we go to Saks, then up to Rumpelmayer's." He tucked her hand into his arm and crossed the wide avenue. "Tonight you have your choice of a musical or a drama, an early dinner or a late supper."

"I'll have to think about it." How long had it been since she'd been so carefree, so unfettered? The man at her side had done that.

"Feel like shopping?" he asked.

Actually she didn't care what they did. Being with him was enough. He was comfortable, exciting, masculine, gentle. Getting to know him was becoming all-important. Her barriers didn't seem that special. "I do feel like shopping," she said. "There used to be a designer on Fifth Avenue who had a shop not far from Bergdorf's. Very interesting clothes—"

"Charine's. She's still there. We'll go."

They strolled up Fifth Avenue, stopping in front of a shop with beige silk curtains on the windows and the name "Charine's" scrolled in gold on the door. Colm almost suggested they not go in. Walking hand in hand with Pacer had more appeal than clothes.

A petite brunette with button black eyes appeared from a back room as soon as Pacer gave his name to a clerk. "Dillon!" she exclaimed. "Where have you been this age, *mon chéri*?"

Pacer bent down to kiss the designer, and Colm felt a funny contraction in her middle.

"I brought a friend to see you," he said. "I knew she'd want your designs over anyone else's."

"*Mais oui.*" Charine smiled at Colm. "Come this way."

Colm hadn't really been that taken with the idea of buying clothes, but immediately changed her mind when she saw the French woman's beautiful designs. After trying on numerous outfits, she finally settled on a silk jumpsuit, a black cocktail dress, and an exquisite gown. Charine promised to have the few needed alterations made on the clothes during the day and deliver them to Pacer's town house later in the afternoon.

"You're annoyed," Pacer said to Colm as they left the shop.

"You didn't have to insist on paying for them. As you know, I do have money."

He hailed a cab and opened the door for her. "Don't be so prickly just because I wanted to give you a few gifts."

"Damned expensive gifts, Dillon."

He followed her into the cab and gave the address of Wendel Towers. "Cool down, Fitzroy. Your honor remains unsullied."

"Dammit—"

Before she could say anything more, she was swept into his arms. She didn't even notice the cab lurching away from the curb as Pacer's mouth fastened on hers, the kiss deepening at once.

Passion whirled through her. In seconds she felt a hot moistness in her lower body. They were in a taxi, for heaven's sake! And she was ready to throw over every warning she'd pounded into her brain just because Pacer Creekwood Dillon held her. Why was he so special? What separated him from other men?

Even as she trembled against him, a part of her tried to hold back. When she felt the throb of his body, her mind went blank.

"Hey, folks," the driver said. "We're here and the meter's running."

"Let it," Pacer muttered.

"Pacer!"

"Yes, darlin'?" He nibbled on her neck.

"Pay the man," she said weakly, then instantly regretted it when he let her go.

Pacer shoved some bills at the driver and turned to Colm.

His hot gaze melted her like wax in the August sun. It stunned her that she had to struggle to keep from throwing herself into his arms.

They walked across the vast lobby of Wendel Towers holding hands. Touching was of prime importance.

As a private elevator sped them to the top floor, Colm glanced at her watch. "We're nearly an hour late. Will that throw off any scheduling?"

Pacer shrugged. "The work will get done by vast groups of efficient people. Con and Dev are incredibly talented." He grinned at her. "Besides, I can't tell you the number of meetings I attended for them because they couldn't leave *their* ladies."

Colm scanned the elevator wall. "Oh?" Was she Pacer's lady?

"My friends are totally taken with their wives." He watched color run up her neck and longed to press his mouth there.

She nodded slowly. "Dev looks like he'd jump off a building for his wife."

"He did."

"What?" Her head snapped up, and she saw his sudden pallor. The hoarseness in his voice revealed a deep emotion. "You're not joking."

"He jumped down a stairwell after a man who was

chasing Felicity," Pacer said colorlessly. "If he had missed the man, he would have fallen twenty stories to his death."

"You saw it," she whispered.

"Yes, and I damn near died on the spot. He's a bloody fool, but he loves Felicity just as Con loves Heller. Con fell in love with Heller almost instantly and moved heaven and earth to care for her when she was in a terrible fire. They love their women." Pacer looked at her. And he loved Colm Fitzroy. When had she taken over his life? It didn't matter. She had.

Colm couldn't turn away from him, just as she couldn't stem the smothering feeling that Pacer Creekwood Dillon was surrounding her, taking her completely. And she wasn't fighting it.

"Pacer, you're a fool." She felt teary, enervated— and she wanted him with an elemental power that awed her. At that moment she could have shoved him to the floor and climbed on top of him. That shocked her.

Her body was sinuous and delightful, Pacer thought. She was a shy Delilah, a winsome Eve. His chest hurt with wanting her.

His body was strong, supple, and so sexy, Colm thought. When had she gone mad? She was day-dreaming about making love with a man she'd known for a week. Yet it seemed right.

"Your eyes are like blue stars," he whispered. "You're very beautiful." He could see the desire in her eyes.

"Yours are like mined silver." She had the strange sensation that he was holding her, loving her. She was insane!

"I like that hoarseness in your voice."

"I must be coming down with something." A terminal case of Pacer Creekwood Dillon. Was he registered with Disease Control?

"Shall I tell you what you do to me?" His blood heated as she stiffened, watching him closely. Her wariness aroused him as he imagined melting all of her resistance.

"Better talk about the business," she muttered. Her head seemed too heavy for her neck. All of her limbs felt leaden, yet she was energized.

He moved toward her and lifted her chin. "You excite my mind, my body, and my spirit, Colm Fitzroy. How and when you did it, I don't know." He kissed her deeply. He'd been slipping through the cracks and hadn't even known it. Colm had stung him to life again. He kissed the pulse in her throat.

"I don't know either," she said. She loved being held by him. He was excitement—and safety. She didn't open her eyes. "Ought to talk about the business." What business?

The elevator doors opened.

Pacer frowned. What were they doing here? They should be back at his house.

"Is this the floor?" she asked.

"Yes, dammit, it is."

"What makes you think we have trouble?"

"There are rumblings, people asking too many questions, records pulled . . ."

"You shouldn't have records."

"Everyone has to tabulate some things. And all this has happened in the last few days. I don't like it."

"Burn anything that would link us to . . . our interests south of the border."

"I will."

"Who are the investigators?"

"Damned if I can find out. That's what makes me leery."

"Government?"

"I don't think so, but they're pros. Been all over the ranch, asking questions in Houston and Dallas."

"Find them and eliminate them."

"I'm trying."

"Do it."

"All right. But you'd better move on your end too."

"I will."

"Who made the call?" Con asked.

"Pacer's people don't identify themselves," Dev said. "You know that."

"Where is the fool?" Con asked idly.

Dev grinned. "You know where he might be. You still pace the floor if you can't get home to Heller early enough."

Con shrugged. "I'm used to the feeling. How about you?"

Dev grinned. "What can I do? Felicity owns me."

"I never saw a happier possession."

"Yeah. And now I think it's happened to Pacer."

Con nodded. "Seems so."

The door to Con's office opened and both men stood as Colm preceded Pacer into the room. "Good *afternoon*," Dev said and grinned when he noticed Colm's pink cheeks and Pacer's possessive glances.

Pacer eyed his friend for a long moment.

Dev closed his eyes. "Call Felicity and tell her that Pacer is going to kill me, Con. She might be able to stop him."

"She and Heller are the only ones who could," Pacer said sweetly.

Con shuddered. "I hate it when you talk in that tone. It reminds me of—" He abruptly stopped speaking.

"What?" Colm asked. "Why are you all looking at each other that way?" She moved nearer to Pacer and took his hand. "Will you tell me?"

Pacer sighed and nodded.

"But he'd rather not," Dev said heavily. "It was my fault."

"Dev."

"Well, it was, Pace." Dev looked Colm square in the eye. "In the last days of Saigon, before the fall, we thought we were home free. One night I was drinking a little too much. Some dudes rolled me, kidnapped me and dumped me in hostile territory. I was captured and put in a bamboo cage. What they did to you in there wasn't nice, but the worst part was that you could neither stand nor sit. It was built for optimum discomfort. Pacer and Con came in to rescue me. Con got me out, but the alarm was given. Pacer killed half a dozen men with his bare hands so that we could get away . . . and he never spoke above a whisper." Dev shot a hard glance at his friend. "He hated doing that, and it wouldn't have been necessary if I hadn't gotten drunk."

"And I told you to forget it."

"You can't. Why should I?"

"Cut it out, both of you," Con said sharply. "Colm doesn't need to hear any more."

Pacer whipped his head around toward Colm, taking in her wide-eyed look, her stiff stance. "Darlin', don't."

"Does anybody really know you?"

"Not completely," Con said. "We come the closest, until now. I have a feeling you'll know much more than we do."

"He's right," Pacer said flatly.

Colm shook her head. "That's hard to believe."

He lifted her off her feet and kissed her, his mouth moving gently on hers.

"We're not the only ones owned by women," Dev said in a low voice to Con.

"True. It's wonderful to see."

"You sound amazed."

"So do you."

Colm opened her eyes. "Pacer, put me down," she said against his lips.

"All right. Temporarily." He let her slide down his body but didn't release her completely. Turning to his friends, he said, "You've heard something."

"Very cryptic, very secretive as usual," Dev said. "It seems that the man in question, Milo Webster, was a close confidant of Vince Collamer. . . ." He glanced at Colm.

"Go on," she said tightly. "I'm aware that my father did business with Webster."

"A lot of it south of the border, way south. Like in Nicaragua and Colombia."

She gasped, her gaze going from Dev to Con. "No one has ever hinted that my father was involved in drugs or arms running, if that's what you're implying, Mr. Abrams."

Dev nodded slowly. "Call me Dev."

"Even the best investigators make mistakes, Colm," Con said.

She faced Pacer squarely. "But you don't think yours did."

"They've been right a good share of the time," Pacer said quietly. "But I agree with Con. The best of them can be wrong." He paused. "Would you rather not hear the rest of this?"

She moved to a chair and seated herself. "I want to know it all."

Dev shot a quick look at Pacer, who nodded, then glanced at Con. Con sat back down behind his desk and picked up a pad.

"It would seem that drugs are only part of it. Smuggling of people into the country is another, plus laundering money through international holding companies." He paused, reading from the pad. "It would seem that the people smuggled in are mobsters from other countries who are listed with Interpol. They're brought into this country and given new identities."

Dev whistled. "This is heavy stuff. Maybe we should inform the government."

"Have your informants discovered that my father was involved in all of this?" Colm asked in a thin voice.

"His name crops up from time to time," Con said, "but there is no hard—"

"My father was Webster's partner in some facets of business, but he was not Webster's only partner."

Con hesitated, tapping the pad. "Did you know that your stock is being bought up by a concern called Ajax Investments?"

She nodded. "I've been trying to buy more shares myself." She inhaled shakily. "To tell the truth, I thought Ajax was connected with AbWenDil."

"No, we are starting to purchase shares . . . at Pacer's directive," Dev said gently.

Colm swallowed. "I trust him." The die was cast. When she saw the blinding smile on Pacer's face, she wanted to kiss him, to hold him. Trying to free herself from his aura, she looked at his friends. "It's funny about Webster in a way."

"In what way?" Dev asked.

"My father once thought I might want to marry him."

Dev saw Pacer's fingers curl around the arms of his chair. "No chance of that."

"Damn right."

"There's that sweet voice again," Con said laconically. "She's here in the room with us, Pace. No harm can come to her."

"Damn right."

"He's having a tantrum," Dev explained gently to a round-eyed Colm. "Anybody foolish enough to cross him now becomes a dirt ball."

"Oh." Colm watched the slight working of Pacer's features, as though someone were remolding him. Reaching out, she clasped his hand and smiled at him.

He lifted her hand and pressed his mouth to it.

Con's mouth dropped open. "Lord, she does have the power."

"Yes," Dev said faintly as he watched Pacer staring at Colm, the tension slowly leaving his body. "What do you want to do?"

Pacer turned to Dev. "Clean out Webster's closets. Find out everything."

Con and Dev stood, and Colm felt she was staring at a war party of two.

"We're going after them," Pacer said conversationally. "Hard and fast, quick and easy."

"Just like that?"

"Yes, Con, just like that."

"All right."

Dev nodded sharply, just once.

Colm stared open-mouthed at Pacer, then at the two men facing him, so calmly accepting. "It sounds like a declaration of war," she said shakily.

"Only if I find out they've been undercutting you, hassling you, darlin' . . . or if they have anything that belongs to you."

"Then I'm in too."

"Of course." He leaned over and kissed her cheek, letting his mouth linger there. "It won't be easy, sweetheart, if they're the kind I think they are. We'll have to play very rough . . . because they will."

She nodded.

Con shook his head, sighing. "I don't suppose there's a chance that any of this could be a tempest in a teapot."

"Maybe," Pacer said. "But I had very bad feelings at the ranch. Nothing we can't handle."

"That tears it," Dev said flatly. "When do we go?"

"Not until I get back to Houston and clear a few paths first."

"Rance," Colm said quietly.

Pacer nodded. "He's one. We'll move easy. We have until the next board meeting of Fitzroy's. In the meantime, I'll show Colm New York and she'll show me Houston. My people will handle the rest . . . when I say go."

"Then we'd better get in position," Dev said. "Colm, we'll be buying more of your stock and doing some in-depth business studies too."

"All right. I'll vote the block of stock I inherited from my mother with you." She smiled faintly. "That's how I elbowed my way to CEO and the presidency." Her smile slipped. "The last few board meetings, Webster's been playing hardball. At first he was very covert, but now he's openly trying to oust me from those positions."

Con nodded. "We'll do our best to change his plans. We'll fly down after you get things rolling, Pace. Until then we'll stay very quiet except for buying the stock. This might be fun."

"Understood." Pacer's benign expression hardened for an instant. "I feel there is much hidden, much that I need to know." He shook his head. "It's there—murky, but there—just under the surface."

Dev whistled softly and Con stiffened.

"What is it?" Colm asked, looking from one to the other.

Dev hesitated. "Pacer . . . sees things. Sometimes it happens when he meets people . . . he sees their deepest secrets." Dev shook his head. "His grandfather Gray Wolf was a mystic."

Colm accepted it fully. Why did she believe in Pacer Creekwood Dillon? She couldn't answer that, but believe she did. "I've had a feeling that I should keep my eyes shut when I look at you." She laughed and touched his cheek. "That's a crazy thing to say, isn't it?"

He captured her hand and again kissed it.

"She's got him by the jugular," Dev said happily.

"Indeed she does." Con smiled when Pacer lifted his head to look at them. "Are we pushing our luck?"

"A little." But Pacer smiled. Simply having Colm near him gave him so much joy! Then the fear struck his mind again. She was in danger! From whom? From what? He'd take care of that, but they couldn't move too fast. He had to know more. For now there was time to be close to Colm, to know her and let her know him. He stroked her cheek.

Colm felt as if his touch had branded her. A wild-fire by the name of Pacer was out of control, burning down to the white heat that would incinerate all her defenses . . . and she was glad. "Are you still going to show me more of New York?"

"Yes."

She'd be safe with him, he thought. And having her in his house made him very happy. "We'll walk Megan in the park after lunch."

"Today?" Somehow the large dog didn't seem threatening any more. Could Pacer take all her fears away?

"Yes."

"And we'll do some buying," Conrad murmured as he picked up the phone on his desk.

Dev got on another line.

"I'll see you," Pacer said quietly.

The other two nodded, already intent on their business.

Colm walked out of the room beside Pacer, quite sure she could have boxed and tied the tension running through him, reached out and grasped it in her hand. Yet she knew if she looked up his expression would be relaxed, serene, calm. Little by little, baby step by baby step, he was tying her to him, taking on her problems. But did she know him?

What would life be without him now? With great effort she controlled the shudder that threatened to run through her. Who was Pacer Creekwood Dillon? Angel? Devil? Savior? Destroyer? All of the above? None?

"Relax, darlin', we're going to enjoy our short vacation."

"I know."

"But you're still not sure of me."

"I'm very sure of the part of you I know, but there's a great deal I don't know." He was a beautiful enigma who made her heart beat faster than it should. In love with a perfect stranger? Nonsense.

"We'll unpeel it together," he said. "Nothing will be hidden from you." Would he be able to peel back the coverings on her troubles? he wondered. Colm Fitzroy had an armor, a sexy, mind-blowing armor.

Colm smiled up at him, but she couldn't help wondering what price Pacer would pay in exposing his inner core to her. Could she open up to him? She was quite sure he had not been totally open with anyone else, not even Dev and Con. Perhaps the price would be too high—for both of them.

Six

New York was magical. They laughed all the time while exploring the glass and steel caves of the sophisticated city.

Colm knew she would never forget her time with Pacer. He'd wrapped her in a golden joy that she had never hoped to have. Could she keep him? She tried to thrust the question from her mind.

The days flew by. The nights were heavenly.

"I didn't think you would like to dance," she said to him one evening as they swayed to a gentle waltz at the Rainbow Room.

"I do now, more than ever." He pressed his mouth to her hair. "Your dress is beautiful on you, but then I've told you that, haven't I?"

"Tell me again." She chuckled. With Pacer there was no attempt to hide herself. He never insisted on knowing more than she was willing to tell him. As a result she'd been more forthcoming with him. It was as though for a few days, in magical Manhattan, they could forget the encroaching world, be cocooned from the mundane. She even went running with Megan and Pacer in Central Park and had begun to like the hairy behemoth that Pacer called an Irish wolfhound.

Trotting behind the dog on the last day in New York, Colm couldn't help laughing when people jumped out of her way. "See?" she said to Pacer. "I told you it would work."

"I don't see it that way. Take her off the leash, Colm. What if she takes off with you?"

"She won't, she's a good girl."

When another dog growled at Megan, the wolfhound paused.

"Hey, lady, keep that lion on a tight rein. My Harvey don't like other dogs." The burly man looked somewhat like his pugnacious dog.

"You hang onto your dog, mister," Colm said. "He's the dangerous one. Come, Megan, I don't want you mixing with riffraff."

"Nice going," Pacer muttered, glancing over his shoulder as they kept jogging.

"I didn't think they let people like that in Central Park." Colm was panting a bit, perspiration coating her body. "Don't you ever sweat or get out of breath?" she asked crossly.

"I would have if I'd had to deck that dog owner back there."

"Nonsense. A mere gnat." Redoubling her efforts Colm tried to pass Pacer, but to no avail. Dropping back, she pulled on Megan and sagged onto a park bench. "You . . . are . . . trying to kill . . . me."

"Your 'mere gnat' might have cost me a few teeth." Pacer sank down next to her, pulling her close. "I won't let you get away from me, Colm," he said and kissed her.

Stars and planets wheeled behind her eyes. Colm finally drew back. "People are watching," she said, gasping.

"Not in Manhattan, darlin'. Kiss me again."

She did. "I wish we didn't have to leave today," she said against his mouth.

"You can show me your city. How's that?"

"All right." Out of breath, out of sync, she stared up at him. Damn, she was enthralled with him. How had it happened?

When they returned to Texas, Colm was still caught in the rosy aura Pacer had wrapped around her.

Houston had the glittering look of the Emerald City in the merry, merry land of Oz as they drove from the airport to Colm's apartment. Sunshine coated it with gold, dotting everything with solar jewels.

"You're nervous," Pacer said, glancing at her.

"What makes you think that?" she asked, her voice as tart as a new apple.

"Is it because I accepted your offer to stay at your place?"

"Don't be silly." With him in her apartment she could make a fool of herself, she thought, beg him to let her climb into his bed. Where had her fear of intimacy gone? In a way she wished it were back.

"If it's any comfort" he said, "I had no intention of letting you stay in your apartment by yourself. I thought I told you I'd gotten funny feelings."

"You did."

"Then don't fret yourself. I'm staying with you."

He drove the Mercedes down into the underground garage, into the space marked with Colm's name, and helped her from the car. "You have wonderful legs, darlin'."

"Thank you." Colm felt as if she were upside down and sideways. Why did it no longer bother her that the hot mysterious Pacer Creekwood Dillon had walked into her life and taken up residence?

Carrying a small bag while Pacer brought the two heavier ones, she walked ahead of him toward the elevator, noticing that he looked intently around the garage. He was always on his guard, she mused. When she heard an engine fire she barely took notice. Her mind was on Pacer—and having him in her apartment. She was halfway to the elevator when a prickling of fear made her pause and turn to face the oncoming car.

It was speeding toward them and, frozen for an instant, Colm could only stare. Then instinct made her muscles tighten, preparing to flee.

Before she could move, Pacer swerved in front of her, pushing her out of the way just as the car reached them. She hit the concrete floor hard. Dazed but aware, she heard a grunt of pain and knew he'd been hit. Pacer was hurt!

Engine roaring, the car raced up the exit ramp and was gone.

Her shoulder and hip ached from the impact of her fall, but Colm ignored the pain as she pushed herself up and turned to Pacer. He was sitting up, rubbing his shoulder.

"Pacer? Are you hurt badly?"

"Just a bump."

"You saved me."

He didn't answer that. "You fell pretty hard. Let me check you over."

"I should be the one checking you. I heard that grunt."

"Why don't we go upstairs and I'll let you go over all of me?"

Heat swept through her. "Very funny."

"I wasn't being funny." He stood and helped her to her feet. "Shall we go?"

When the elevator doors closed behind them, reaction began setting in. Colm started shaking and turned to Pacer.

"That car," she said weakly, "was aiming for . . ."

"Shh." He pulled her into his arms. "Don't think about it. I'm here with you. I'll keep you safe." His hands stroked her back, smoothing away the shivers. "No one's going to hurt you."

She lifted her head, blindly seeking his mouth, his warmth and strength. His tongue thrust between her lips, jousting gently with hers.

Her arms encircled his waist, her hands digging in, holding him. She wanted him to love her. The last of the barriers around her heart caved in and she pressed even closer to him.

Pacer's heart thudded against his chest so hard, it felt as though it would burst through. He drew her up his body, wanting her with a need that transcended all else. "Darlin', I'll be taking you in this elevator—and I'd like more privacy for what I want to do."

His words torched her. "Sounds interesting."

"Doesn't it?" Desire pulsated through him. He wanted her, but he cherished her, too, needed to protect her. There was eagerness in her eyes, but there was a lingering trepidation as well.

The elevator stopped on Colm's floor. The doors opened at the same moment the door to her apartment opened, revealing her housekeeper, Pina, standing there with a large iron skillet in her hand.

"Señorita? Is it you?" Pina asked.

"Good thing we waited," Pacer said mildly.

"Yes, Pina." Colm laughed as Pacer released her reluctantly. "What are you doing?"

"Protecting myself, señorita," Pina said, gesturing for Colm and Pacer to go into the apartment. "I have bought a *perro* as well."

"Dog? You bought a . . ." Colm's voice faded as she glimpsed the beast standing in her foyer.

"An Irish wolfhound, like Megan," Pacer said. "How fitting. Hey, boy . . ."

"It is a girl, señor, her name is Pansy. She lives here now." Pina looked at Colm. "I know of your fears, señorita, but she is better than the alarm system. That is why she must live here."

"I see," Colm said faintly. It was one thing to live with Megan in Pacer's town house for a few days, and quite another to have this wolfhound in her own apartment. Still, she saw the merit in what Pina had said. "I suppose she is better than a burglar alarm."

"Sí. She cannot have her wires cut, señorita."

"True."

"She seems friendly enough," Pacer said, putting his hand out to the dog to let her sniff.

"She is—unless you try to hit me, señor. Then she would kill you." Pina beamed. "My cousin Juan, he say she is well trained. And he will train her to protect Señorita Colm too."

"Juan has trained racing dogs in Florida," Colm explained to Pacer. "Now he has a business in Houston training guard dogs."

"*Sí*, and he tell me that she has too much heart to be a killer but she will protect you and me, señorita, so I took her."

"Uh, fine. But I'd rather she didn't kill Señor Dillon either, Pina."

Pina shrugged. "Well, maybe she won't."

"Comforting." Pacer smiled and hunkered down, the big wolfhound nuzzling against him. "And Juan knows enough to be sure this dog will protect the house, Pina?"

"*Sí*. Juan is a good trainer, señor."

"Her cousin is an . . . entrepreneur of sorts," Colm said dryly. "He's also been known to run a cockfight or two and smuggle high-grade tequila across the border."

"My family is not proud of that part of Juan . . . but sometimes he is useful," Pina said, tight-lipped. "And the dog was purchased, señorita. I told your uncle to pay Juan."

"Uncle Henry?"

"*Sí*."

"But why, all of a sudden, do we need a dog?"

"I'd like to know the answer to that one," Pacer said sweetly, turning Colm's head toward him. Her skin prickled as she recognized the tone of voice that had so startled Dev and Con.

"Someone broke into the apartment," Pina said. "I called the *policía* afterwards and when they came I was hiding." Pina's mouth hardened. "Those bad men tore apart the study, pulled every book from the shelves. Some of them were damaged. I will not have such things here." Pina gestured with the heavy skillet. "I do not take this in a bed."

"Lying down," Colm corrected her softly.

"*Sí*, that is what I said. They couldn't get into the safe, but they tried."

"Oh? There's nothing in the safe."

"Why didn't you call us?"

Pina stared at Pacer for a long moment. "You think they might come back again. Is that it?"

"Maybe. Let me look at the study."

"After the *policía* left, I cleaned it. They said that I could."

"Damn." Pacer winced, then nodded. "I'll just take a look anyway."

Colm watched him stride across the marble foyer. Then she looked at Pina and the dog. "Here, Pansy." What a silly name for the giant animal!

As the dog pressed her nose into her hand, Colm studied the closed study door.

"*Mucho hombre*, señorita. I am glad he is here with you."

"So am I." Colm looked down at the dog, whose face was not that far below hers. "I'm glad you're here too, Pansy."

Pacer walked around the study, touching things, running his fingers over the books, but there were no vibrations. Pina, clean housekeeper that she was, had scrubbed away any vestige of the intruders. What were they after? What had spooked them into going after Colm now? Upheaval in the company? Possible takeover? What? Why now?

Pacer's blood seemed to drain from his body. Fear such as he'd never known shook him. Damn them all to hell, he'd find out who was after her—and why.

He picked up the phone and dialed a number. "Yes, it's Pacer. They hit Colm Fitzroy's apartment. I don't know what they were looking for, but I'm going to find out. And she was narrowly missed in the parking garage. Go over it. Now. Do it. I want to know everything by this evening. You heard me. And put people in this building and at Fitzroy's . . . and more at the ranch. Don't forget Rance Caleb."

He replaced the phone and walked around the room again, trying to imagine what the interlopers had been seeking.

Colm opened the door and froze in place. Pacer was standing in the center of the room, his eyes closed, clenched fists at his sides, barely breathing.

"It's all right, darlin'. Come in."

"How did you know it was me?"

"I'll always know when you're near me."

"I called Rance on another line. He's coming in— reluctantly. I told him you would shoot him if he didn't."

"I'll shoot anybody who puts you in harm's way. And if Webster and his bunch were behind this break-in, I'll take them down hard," he said simply.

"You seemed convinced it was they."

"Pretty much."

"But what?"

He smiled. "You're beginning to read me, sweetheart. I like that." His smile faded. "There's something about all this that doesn't ring true, darlin'. I don't know what it is . . . but I will."

"You think someone else is involved?"

He moved his shoulders as though he carried a heavy weight on them. "I don't know what it is, but something bothers me, and I'd be a fool not to pay attention to it."

She nodded. "I called Uncle Henry to offer to pay for the dog, but he wouldn't let me. He's coming over for dinner tonight."

"He's a good man. Has a fine reputation in business."

"He could have had any number of businesses on his own, but he's always been loyal to Fitzroy's." She smiled. "He was a very close friend of my mother's . . . and I think his wife was, too, but I never knew her. She died just before I was born. But he tells me many stories about my mother."

"Didn't your father do that?" Pacer watched her features change, harden.

"I never asked my father about my mother." She bit her lip. "He never loved her, he couldn't have. I didn't understand everything he said to her, but I can still see her face, all tight and pain-ridden. As young as I was, I knew that he hit her at times. Mother would explain the bruises by saying that she fell." Colm lifted her eyes to Pacer's. "I don't recall a time when I wanted to be in my father's company." She turned away. "I can still recall the many times he would bring women to the house while my mother was alive. I was quite young when she died, but I remember the women."

"It might have been business, darlin'."

Colm whirled to face him. "No. They weren't business associates, because his women were in the house day and night. And after Mother died it was worse. Before I even started school I knew about them. Some of his women made nasty little remarks that cut me, so I learned to avoid them, but I knew they were there.

"When my governesses complained about the partying and drinking, the bad atmosphere for a child, he fired them. Eventually he sent me away to boarding school." She gulped back a sob. "As frightened as I was, I knew it was better than being at home."

Pacer moved fast to her, cuddling her close to him. "You won't be lonely ever again. I'll be with you." He leaned back from her. "Our children won't be sent off to school until they're ready . . . and the only thing they'll see is the two of us canoodling."

Colm laughed shakily. "You've just taken two giant steps, Dillon." His child! Streaky blond hair, silver-blue eyes, fearless at two years old—stop!

"It helps to have long legs," he told her silkily, one hand massaging her spine. "You're beautiful."

Heat swept through her like a cyclone, stealing her breath. "We should get ready for dinner. We're having guests."

"Yes." Flames licked over his skin, through his flesh, melting him to her. "Will you let me take you upstairs and love you?"

"Yes." It was foolish, possibly dangerous. "Yes, I will."

They walked out into the hall and mounted the stairs side by side.

She wasn't going to a hanging, she told herself. She was going to a loving. She was just jittery, that was all.

"No pressure, darlin'," Pacer said.

"I know." She led him into her room. The familiar champagne and coral decor seemed alien. She walked straight to the bed and sat down because her legs were too wobbly to support her. "Here we are."

Pacer knelt in front of her. "Any time you say halt, we will, darlin'."

"Kiss me, Pacer. Take the fear away."

Did she recall that she'd said that same thing to him in New York? he wondered. "Oh, darlin', I'll try."

He laid her back on the bed, then undressed her slowly, kissing her time after time. Then he rose, ripping off his own clothes and scattering them.

Kneeling on the bed he bent over her middle, blowing across her bare skin. She gasped and he placed his mouth there, his tongue touching, laving, massaging the delicate flesh.

Passion rocked him, blood hammered through his veins, bringing him to a readiness he struggled to tamp. With all his soul he wanted to please her, make her spill over in love. His mouth whorled over her skin, branding her, his tongue taking her, telegraphing his feelings, his desires to her in sweet questing.

"Silly me, I thought tongues were for talking." Colm was out of breath and feeling as though she was flying around the room weightless.

"Among other things." He spoke against her skin, sparking a slow heat that matched the one consuming him. His head moved downward, his mouth moving aside her satin panties even as his hand came up to pull them gently down and off.

"Pacer!"

"I'm loving you, sweet Colm. Relax."

"Like this?"

"Like this. You'll like it, you'll see."

"Oh." Fire pierced her like a million darts when she felt his velvet intrusion, the warm, hot, sweet, brand-new invasion of her body. Gentle, explosive, calming, exciting, all the sensations were one in her as Pacer loved her. She blew apart and came together again as part of him. Awesome, overwhelming . . .

Heat seared her, bucking her body, arching her into him. All of Pacer's soothing caresses could not quench the flame as her being took fire. "Now!" she cried from the depths of her being, not even knowing she'd spoken.

"Darlin'. . ." Pacer's face appeared above hers, his hair tousled, his eyes half-closed yet glittering with excitement.

"I didn't know," she said weakly, her fingers digging into his shoulders. She blinked at him. "It's wonderful."

"Yes."

"Love me."

"I have from the moment I held your dress together. I will forever." The words bound them, a sweet covenant building into a hot aura. Slowly his mouth and hands moved over her, once more bringing her to the edge of fire.

The heat pulsed through her, her body seeming to melt, the dampness of her skin echoed in her lower body. She clung to Pacer. Impatient at his languorous pace, eager for his raw sexuality, she caressed him feverishly.

"You needn't be afraid, my Colm."

"I'm not." And it was true. She was aflame for him, wanting him. She held him to her as her body undulated in invitation.

Pacer couldn't hold back. His body slid into hers, past the moist barrier, the hot casing of her flesh imprisoning him, taking him to an ecstasy previously unknown. "Colm!"

"Yes!" Shocked and shuddering, she climbed the

mountain and exploded over the precipice, tumbling into space, falling into the velvet abyss of lovers.

"I love you."

Who said it?

Pacer held her until the last tremors of love had dissipated.

"I liked that very much," Colm said. She looked up at him, seeing on his face the lazy satisfaction she felt. "It was wonderful. I expected to have some fear. Instead I had only joy."

He smiled. "No one's ever said a nicer thing to me."

"That I'm not frightened of you?"

"Yes, darlin', that means everything to me." Leaning down he took her mouth, fiercely gentle, swallowing the moan that had risen in her throat.

Tongue touching tongue, they swayed in the grip of the passion that rose again like a tropical storm. The magic was taking them once more.

The rush of passion rocked Pacer. Only with Colm could the desire have flared so quickly.

For a flash in time Colm felt a darkness in her soul, then it was gone. Would the happiness be fleeting too? She clung to Pacer.

"I'll always be here with you, Colm."

"Is it so easy to read me?"

"No, darlin'. It's just that we're in tune. I've never been more relaxed with anyone. Our lovemaking is intense, serene and beautiful."

"Crazy, isn't it?" Her eyes fluttered closed as the heat began to build. Why had no one told her it could happen so fast? Lovemaking was astounding and so . . . comfortable. Wonderful. "Good thing we have air conditioning, Pacer Creekwood Dillon, or we'd both be incinerated in the fires you start."

"You're the incendiary one. I'm the calm one in this lovemaking partnership." He kissed her bared breast, feeling anything but calm. His heart thudded against his breastbone. "If you like, we could discuss the stock market." He sucked her nipple into his mouth, savoring the sweetness as his body demanded release.

"Or the price of hogs on the open market." Colm's words were slurred as she touched and took hold of his aroused body. "You certainly respond well to conversation."

"Isn't that the truth. Now about the prices at Rent-A-Wreck." Pacer felt his control slipping. "Nothing we can't talk about, darlin'." What had he just said?

"Lovemaking takes on new meaning if we exchange ideas. Recipes maybe?" Colm was fainting, her voice weak as Pacer's mouth explored her abdomen and lower . . . lower.

"Yes." What had Colm said? Did she speak? His hearing was failing, his eyes glazing over. All banter fled at the feel of the woman he held in his arms. He gave over all power to her. "I love you, darlin'."

"Too soon to know."

"I knew when I held your dress together the first night."

"Snap decision," she said mistily, arching her body to his when he kissed her most intimately.

"I've been riding a lightning bolt since that night."

Wanting with a driving need to give him pleasure, Colm let her mouth rove over his chest, satisfied when he stiffened as she licked his nipples. It had been so easy to learn to love him. "I do like this."

He moved her beneath him, then he slid down her body, beginning at her toes to love her. Moving slowly, he took her in every elemental way a man can, her shuddering body echoing the shaking of his.

In a thrashing crescendo they rose, clinging, twisting, held together as they sailed out beyond the world to the planet they created. Love and life burst around them.

Colm felt a thrust of sweetness that had her gasping. For a moment she was sure she had separated from him and was floating to the stars.

In an explosion of love they took each other, the life force thrusting beyond all their powers, exuding the superpotency of love.

With slow, gentle shudders they sank back.

"My, my, that was wondrous."

"Open your eyes, love."

"No, Pacer, I want to watch the fantasy that's still going on behind my eyes."

"Seeing stars and planets."

Her eyes shot open. "Yes. Are you reading my mind again?"

"No, that's what happens to me when I love you."

She cuddled close to him, just as there was a knock on her bedroom door. Her gaze flew to the vermeil clock chiming six on the wall. "Good Lord, we've been up here for two hours."

"Great things need to be savored," Pacer said as the knock became more peremptory.

"Señorita Colm?"

"Uh, what is it, Pina?"

"*Qué*? Open the door. I wish to discuss the dessert with you."

"That'll teach you to keep old family retainers," Pacer whispered.

Colm glared at him as he lay back with his hands

behind his head. "Her mother was my mother's house-keeper for years, and her grandmother was my mother's nurse. Pina knew my mother very well. Besides, I had no choice. She just arrived here one day and said that she would be staying." Colm was babbling and scrambling for her clothes, getting madder by the second at Pacer, who continued to chuckle as he pulled on his own pants.

Stumbling, Colm charged to the door and opened it a crack. "Just make what you choose, Pina."

"Why are your clothes so messy?" Pina managed to stick her head in the door. "Ah, now I see. It is time you were married."

"About the dessert . . ."

"*Sí*, we will speak of that, but Señor Pacer will marry you anyway."

Pacer could tell from the sound of Colm's voice that she was embarrassed. Smiling, he walked over to the door. He leaned around Colm and said to Pina, "I was making love to her."

"*Sí*," the housekeeper said sternly. "Are you going to marry the señorita? Because if you are not, my cousin Juan will put a bullet in you."

"Pina!" Colm was caught between laughter and tears. "Pacer, be quiet!"

"Bring your cousin around. I would like someone to force us to the altar. This lady is dragging her feet."

"*Qué*?" Pina put her hands on her hips. "So I will get out your mama's wedding veil."

"Good idea," Pacer said promptly. "I'm ready to do the right thing."

Pina nodded. "See, señorita, he fears Juan."

"Ye-es, I can see he does." Colm glared at the

beaming Pacer. "I'm going to shower and get dressed now."

"Me too." He looked back at Pina. "About dessert. I like baked Alaska."

"*Qué?* I made melon ice cream, señorita, but I can . . ."

"Melon ice cream is perfect," Colm said. Pina nodded and left, and Colm shot one more hard look at Pacer. "You had better get going."

"I would've told Pina I like melon ice cream too."

"Peachy." Colm felt hot and cold all at once. She still wanted him. Lord!

"No, melon," Pacer said mildly.

"You are in the room down the hall."

"Probably, but I'd like to move in here." He gazed at her. "Since you'll be making an honest man of me in a few days, I figure it'll be all right."

Colm fought the smile that was lurking inside her. "You're disruptive."

"Me?"

"You."

He walked over to her closets and pressed the button, sliding the doors back. "No room for me here. Maybe I'd better use the room down the hall."

She longed to ask him to stay with her, but it was too soon for that. "The other room is . . . quite comfortable," she said hesitantly.

Smiling, he walked over to her and slid his arms around her waist. "Don't worry about it, darlin'. We have all the time in the world ahead of us." He dropped a kiss on her forehead.

"I'll be going out to the ranch tomorrow morning."

"I'll be with you."

"Tomorrow you have a board meeting at Fitzroy's.

You have to be there. You and I both know the place is in a shaky position fiscally. Do you want to risk a takeover?"

"No." But she'd lose it all, gladly, before she'd give up Pacer.

"Darlin', nothing is going to part us, I promise you." He paused. "Besides, I want you to go over your office with a fine-tooth comb. There could be a secret hiding place somewhere that is holding something the interlopers were trying to locate."

"Could there be another break-in?"

"Could be. More importantly, I want to guard against another incident with a car. I've got people stationed here and at Fitzroy's." He smiled down at her. "In fact, you now have a rather lugubrious assistant by the name of Lazarus. Don't fear him, darlin'. He'll be all over you like a blanket if there's any trouble. And you might notice a few other new staff members as well." Pacer inhaled deeply. "I took a chance on your uncle Henry. Oh, I know you think he's honest, darlin', and I appreciate that, but . . . I had to know for myself. People on the inside give him high marks too."

"Inside?"

Pacer shook his head slowly. "As you already know, I have a network of people, an international group. Some are vets, some are Asian nationals, some are Europeans, but we help one another no matter what. It's active in every kind of profession and business, and we even have second generation personnel."

"Mercenaries?"

"If need be, but that's not the primary function."

"This is the secret army that your friends alluded to?"

"Yes."

She studied his hard features. "Don't push me to one side and go into danger."

"I'm not doing that, even though the thought of you in danger is enough to freeze me solid. I just need to get onto the ranch—by myself. I might even take Pansy with me."

"You've just met her, and you trust her."

"She's like you, my sweet. She has heart."

Colm rubbed her head against his jaw. "Did you just call me a bitch?"

"A very lovely one, maybe." Pacer chuckled. She had so damned much heart. Colm had many fears but she struggled to pigeonhole them, keep them in line. She wanted to support him, even though there were times when she was almost immobilized by the fears that riddled her life. The lady was noble, with a very special grit.

"Monster." She turned her head and bit him on the chin.

"If you think that puts me off, love, don't," Pacer said hoarsely. "Your bite is very arousing."

"Everything arouses you."

"Everything you do."

She looked up and grinned.

He saw the fear behind the front. "I'll come back to you."

"You have to . . . or I'll sue you for breach of promise."

"No need. I'll be back and in your pocket in no time."

"Promise."

"I give you my word."

"Better keep it." When her voice broke she buried her face in his chest.

Pacer could see Colm's face in front of him as he flew the helicopter out to the ranch. She was never far from his thoughts.

He turned to look at the Irish wolfhound beside him. Pansy had had no hesitation about getting into the chopper. "We're almost there, girl."

The dog gazed soulfully at him.

"Ah, there it is. Rance's place. Down we go. Can't let them know we're in the area just yet."

Pacer landed in the small glade he'd used before. The helicopter wouldn't be easily seen there, even from the air. The dog followed him out, staying beside him. Checking the area around the cabin, Pacer saw all was quiet. Even though Rance hadn't liked leaving his place, Pacer was relieved the older man was now in Houston with Colm.

Colm! When he thought of last night, Pacer's body crackled with desire. She'd come to him! He recalled how surprised he'd been when she'd opened his bedroom door.

"I wasn't sure you were coming to my room," she had said softly, "so I decided to come to yours."

He had watched the blood run up her face. Though they'd made love, she was still hesitant and shy with him. "I was coming to yours, darlin', and I was hoping you'd welcome me." He'd held out his arms and she'd glided into them. "I'm on fire for you."

"I feel the same," she'd murmured, coiling her arms around his neck, her mouth parting on his. "I like lovemaking."

"And that's a surprise?"

"Yes."

He had taken her to his bed and they'd loved all night, not falling asleep in each other's arms until shortly before dawn.

Pacer didn't know he'd tightened his hand on Pansy's collar until she made a sound in her throat. "Sorry, girl, I was thinking about your owner. Not a wise thing to do at the moment, but it's hard to put her out of my mind." Pacer chuckled. "I am crazy, carrying on a conversation with a wolfhound. Let's go, girl. We have work to do."

Colm tried to keep her mind on her breakfast and the conversation she was having with Rance, but Pacer was uppermost in her mind. Was he all right? Had he thought last night as beautiful as she? Her being glowed when she remembered the night of passionate giving they'd shared. Pacer was a generous and gentle lover. Just the thought of him kissing her toes made her blood boil. "Pardon me? I'm sorry, Rance, I was daydreaming."

"Knew that. Must be all the damned noise and confusion around here."

"You can take city life for a short while."

"Can't. Hate it. Always did."

Colm looked sternly at the man who'd been more than father, more than friend. "Well, you'll just have to get used to it," she said tartly. "I have enough to worry about with Pacer out there."

"Should be with him." Rance scowled at his pipe. "He don't know Boru land like I do."

"That's what I told him." Dread crawled over her skin, despite the many lectures she gave herself. Pacer was capable. He'd fought in Vietnam. He was cagey, sharp, unafraid. But all her reasoning could not stem the fear.

"I'll be back before you miss me, darlin'." He'd said that just before he'd kissed her hard.

"What if you're not?" It had been difficult to release her hold on him.

"Talk to Dev and Con. They should be here today." Another kiss only sharpened her desire . . . and fear.

Colm toyed with her dish of orange slices. "Do you think there could be trouble? Pacer might be moving too fast."

"He's pretty slick. He should get in and out easy enough." Rance set his unlit pipe down and sipped some orange juice.

"But you don't like it."

"No, I don't like it," Rance said crabbily. "He hasn't dealt with Webster's people. I have."

"Pacer . . . is capable." Losing him would be like dying.

Rance glanced at Colm. "He'd better come back here. I always intended to see you married. Adaira wouldda liked that. Should be a nice weddin', so he'd better get back here, or I'll take my shotgun to 'm."

Colm's smile was wobbly. "That might send him screaming into the night."

"You know it won't."

"Yes, I do." She had never been so sure of anything. Last night had proved that. There was no place to hide even if she had wanted to, and she didn't. If it wasn't love that Pacer felt, she would take whatever it was, because nothing and no one had ever given her the joy that he had. It was more than enough. Last night he'd whispered magical things. She wanted to hear more, to tell him wondrous things as well.

Even now, when they were separated, she had the sensation of kissing him, of being held by him. She needed him!

•   •   •

As Pacer returned to the chopper and unloaded his small knapsack, his errant thoughts touched on Colm.

When the dog growled low in her throat, he grabbed his gun and ran for a nearby thicket. "Come on, girl." Pacer wasn't totally sure she would follow him, but she moved quickly and quietly at his side.

From his vantage point in the thicket, he watched two men approach the cabin warily, guns out, one with a knife in his left hand as well.

"He musta gone huntin'," one said.

"Yeah. Lucky for him," the man with the knife said. "We wouldda hadda kill him otherwise."

"Wouldn'ta minded. The old coot chased me once, put a round a' salt in my backside."

"Yeah, well now you can burn his place down. That should help some."

"It will."

Pacer hadn't wanted to show his hand, but neither could he let them burn Rance's place. "Well, my girl," he whispered to the wolfhound, "we're going to test just how well you can do."

Crawling slowly out of the thicket, Pacer fixed on the one with the fuel can. When the man became absorbed in laying a trail of gasoline at the base of the cabin, Pacer ran up behind him, springing at him and catching the man off guard.

Pacer struck with one hand, bringing the other up to jam the man's mouth shut to prevent sound.

The man's surprised grunt sounded loud in the stillness. Pacer had to hope it hadn't been heard by the other man.

He heard the dog's growl and the running footsteps at the same time. He turned and saw the butt of the rifle descending toward his skull.

At the same time, Pansy launched herself into the air, taking man and gun to the ground. The weapon discharged mightily, but the dog tore at her adversary as though nothing had interrupted them.

Pacer turned in time to dispatch the first man, who was coming to.

"Good girl. Watch them."

Returning to the chopper, Pacer radioed one of his men. "I got a couple here that need picking up. What? Webster's been busy, hasn't he? And he hasn't registered with the SEC? Well, I think we'd better put a stop to his stock buying. Where the hell is he getting the money to make a run like this? Take care of things. I'm going in."

Pacer tied the men in the shade of the cabin, giving them each a drink of water before gagging them. "Don't worry. You'll be picked up in fifteen or twenty minutes. Then it's off to a comfortable jail cell."

Both men glared at him, muttering behind the gags.

Returning to the thicket he picked up his bag and gun, then headed for the well-worn path that would take him onto the huge spread.

The dog padded easily at his side as Pacer broke into a trot, covering ground swiftly as he'd been trained to do as a child.

A little over an hour later he was looking down on the ranch house. "Damn, it's a beautiful place, set in those rolling hills. A Texas Eden."

The dog whined softly.

"Good girl." Pacer patted her head. "Why don't you

stay here? Stay." He started forward, staying low. In his peripheral vision he saw the dog hunch her body down and follow him. "All right. It's the two of us."

Colm didn't relish attending the board meeting. Her mind was on Pacer. It helped to have Rance at her side, and she smiled when he edged a chair next to hers at the head of the long table, ignoring the raised eyebrows of a member or two.

At first the meeting moved slowly, the atmosphere cautious and friendly. But step by step those not averse to a takeover made their feelings known. And Milo Webster was their spokesman.

"I resent the implication, Mr. Webster," Colm said coldly, "that I'm not able to handle the company that belongs to me."

Webster smiled thinly. "Your father had no plans for you taking over his—"

"Fitzroy's was in my mother's family, not my father's, Mr. Webster."

Webster moved his shoulders dismissively. "Nonetheless, since he and I were partners and he entrusted me with his voting shares, I think you are just marking time, hoping you'll come up with a solution to your problems. You won't, Ms. Collamer."

"The name is Fitzroy, as you well know, and as you have called me in the past."

"I hope you don't mean to insult your father's name, Ms. . . . er, uh, Fitzroy."

"What I mean can be no concern of yours, Mr. Webster. Though I will tell you I'm well aware of your buying Fitzroy stock through Ajax Investments. I can assure you it will in no way deter me from my

goal of putting Fitzroy's at the top of the fiscal charts."
She inhaled shakily when she saw Webster's eyes
narrow. He reminded her of a snake. "Now, shall
we get back to the business at hand. Perhaps if the
secretary would read the last *pertinent* statement . . ."

Around and around it went, back and forth. Colm
didn't give an inch, but Webster was waging a strong
insider game, inexorably pushing her into a fiscal
corner with his sharp questions. Where had he gained
so much detailed information about Fitzroy's? she
wondered time and again.

When the door opened quietly and two tall, well-
groomed men entered, Colm turned. "Dev, Con."
Relief coursed through her when she saw their smiles.
They would help Pacer. Then maybe she could con-
centrate on beating Milo Webster at his own game.

"What do you want?" Webster blustered. "This is a
gathering of board members who will be voting to—"

"Oh?" Dev interrupted smoothly. "Well, since we
have voting control over a block of the stock, we
would want to be in on this." He smiled pleasantly.
"You do want us to vote our stock with yours, don't
you, Ms. Fitzroy?"

Colm nodded as a shiver raced down her back.
Had they been able to procure enough shares? If so,
how had they managed that so quickly?

"And," Con added, "we have decided to throw all
our votes behind Ms. Fitzroy's changes and improve-
ments. Fitzroy's will be having an overhaul of sorts,
but many of her policies will remain in effect, such
as the rehiring of laid-off employees and other innovative proposals." His smile widened when he saw
Colm's pleased surprise. "Shall we get on with it?"

There was no contest. Milo Webster was routed. When the voting was over, Dev sat back in his chair and smiled coolly at Webster.

"If you're interested in selling your shares, Webster, call this number." He pushed a card across the table to Webster. "We'll give you fair market value." Dev named a figure that made Webster grind his teeth.

"We'll see about this," Webster said, glaring at Dev and Con.

"Don't try anything fancy, Webster," Dev said quietly. "We might just feel it's time to release our dossier on you."

Webster whitened for a moment, then rallied. "I have a few dossiers of my own. Maybe it's time I showed mine around."

"Get out of here," Con said in a low voice.

Webster opened his mouth, shut it again, then shoved his chair back and strode out of the room.

"That's the first time I've ever seen anyone apoplectic," Dev said, leaning down and kissing Colm on the cheek. "I've always wanted to use that word."

"You're a fighter, Colm Fitzroy," Con said. "I think you chased him home." His eyes narrowed as she bolted out of her chair. "What's the matter?"

"He'll go back to Boru. Pacer's there."

"Is he?" Con said softly. "And he told me he'd be around when we arrived. I owe him one for this."

"Let's roll," Dev said harshly. "I'm doing the flying."

Colm shot a quick look at him as she walked with the two men to the elevator. "Pacer says you're a hotshot pilot."

"Coming from Pace, that's a joke."

"Dev can be scary from time to time," Con said

mildly. "Today we could use that, I think." He exchanged a glance with Dev as the elevator took them to the roof. "Can you beat Webster there?"

"I can beat him anywhere—and if not, I'll shoot him down," Dev said grimly. "He won't get Pacer."

Con nodded.

"If Webster harms Pacer . . ." Colm began. Her voice broke and she took a deep, steadying breath. Pacer was tough, she told herself. He would be all right. He'd come back to her. He'd promised.

"He won't get Pacer, Colm," Con said. "Few people could. It would be tragic for Houston if anything happened to Pacer anyway."

"What do you mean?"

"This 'secret army' of Pacer's . . . They're all very loyal to him. If something happened to Pacer, they might level Houston."

"Oh."

"And we'd help them." There was the sound of doomsday in Dev's voice.

"Me too," Colm said. "I can't lose him."

The two men looked at her and nodded.

Seven

Pacer was on a knoll, the dog at his side.

A guard had passed not two feet from where he lay on his stomach, peering down at the ranch. "Good girl." Pacer patted the wolfhound, who had never moved or growled. "Let's go."

In a crouch, he ran quickly and quietly from cover to cover, the dog at his heels.

In the last bit of thicket that edged the small clearing in front of the house, he straightened, brushed himself off, and watched. When he was sure no one was around, he strolled out of the brush and unhurriedly made his way to the front door.

He and Pansy walked in as though they were invited guests. Drawing on his knowledge of large ranch houses—which was somewhat limited—he opted to try the second door down the wide center hall. Taking a deep breath, he turned the knob and pushed the door open. He'd guessed right. It was Webster's study, and it was empty.

Pressing his back against the door, he looked for hidden equipment that would tell him an electronic scan system was functioning. He saw nothing. He would have to take a chance that the room wasn't scanned. Webster probably didn't think it necessary to monitor his own office, anyway.

The dog pushed her muzzle into his hand and whined softly. "Good girl, Pansy. Let me know if someone is coming."

Pacer scrutinized the bookshelves, the desk, the obvious painting that could mask a safe. Would Webster keep his most precious papers in his bedroom or here? No matter. He was in the study, he would look here first.

When he spotted the book ladder, he followed the track around, studying the types of books. Maps, charts, investment data, fiscal tomes of varying sizes and shapes. . . .

He walked over to the desk, opening the locked drawers easily. Nothing.

The picture over the mantel couldn't be budged.

He checked the drapes, the carpet, even the bar. Nothing.

"We have to go upstairs, girl."

He opened the door a crack and saw a stout, dark-haired woman walk down the wide passageway. Waiting a second after she disappeared, he crossed the hall to the staircase and ran up it.

Relying purely on instinct he chose a set of double doors that he hoped would open to the master suite. The other doors opening off the stucco-walled passage were single ones. Locked! In seconds his handy burglar's tool had popped the lock and he and the dog were inside.

Moving faster now but trying to disturb little, he tapped the walls and looked through the many chests and closets. Nothing! What the hell?

When the dog growled low in her throat he turned, then stalked to the window. "Helicopter," he muttered. "Won't be Con or Dev coming in that way."

There were places to hide in the study. He wanted Webster alone when he choked some information out of him.

Keeping the dog with him, Pacer left the bedroom and peered over the balustrade to the large foyer. He saw no one and started down. The dark-haired woman spotted him when he was halfway to the first floor. He kept his hand on Pansy, his gaze locked on the woman.

"You are the man of Señorita Colm, no?" she asked in accented English.

He nodded once, realizing this woman must be the housekeeper and was still loyal to the Fitzroys.

"He will kill you."

"I'll hide in the study."

"He'll come there."

"I know."

"Hide behind the bar. He never lets anyone use it."

"Thank you."

As Pacer hurried down the stairs and into the study, the housekeeper bolted the front door. When she saw the study door close behind Pacer, she unlocked the front door. Señorita Colm had a hero, she thought. He would make sure Boru was returned to her.

Then the front door was flung open, the ornate oak banging against the wall.

The housekeeper stiffened at the sound, her lips

tightening. Then she melted into the semidarkness of the hallway. Hiding from Milo Webster had become a habit.

"Let's get the files out, Brice," Webster said, striding into the house. "I want to know everything about those two."

"I can tell you that Conrad Wendel and Deveril Abrams are tough men," Brice said. "If you tangle with them, you could lose."

"I don't lose, Brice. Remember that."

Brice shrugged. "Maybe you should think about taking Troy up on his offer. We could get out of here. Go to the place in Mexico."

"No. I like it here . . . and it cost me plenty to get this place."

"Troy approached me before the meeting. The offer was better."

"The answer's still no, Brice. I'm staying here. Boru's mine." Webster paused, staring into space. "Funny. Why would he want it so bad? What's he up to?" He waved a hand as though to erase his thoughts. "To hell with him." He looked around him and smiled. "When I was a kid growing up, I'd see the planes taking off from rich bastards' places while I was mucking out their stables. I said I'd be there myself someday. I am, and Boru makes that statement for me. I'm staying."

Brice stayed Webster's hand when the other man opened the door to his study. "Troy is going to call this afternoon."

"Put him off."

"All right. One more thing. You said you wanted to take a look at the new mare."

"Yeah. The one thing I know is horseflesh. If that

bastard dealer tried to cheat me, I'll know it in a minute. Where've you got her?"

"In the north stable."

"Let's go, but make it fast. I want to get Claus and Stefan on this. They're the types we need to take down the hard-noses."

"I don't trust either of them."

Webster's laughter was like a bark. "You don't have to like them. All that matters is that they do their job."

Pacer heard the door shut again and the voices fade away. No one had come into the study. Waiting precious seconds to be sure, he lifted his head to peer over the edge of the bar. It was going to be damn hard to hide the dog. "Come, girl." Opening the hall door again, he saw the housekeeper. "Can you keep her in the kitchen?" At the woman's nod, he smiled. "If it gets . . . noisy in here, you hide, but turn her loose."

"Sí, señor, but I have a rolling pin. Hurry, you must hide." Speaking in rapid Spanish to the dog, the housekeeper urged Pansy to go with her.

It was only when Pacer spoke sharply to the animal that she followed the housekeeper.

Pacer reentered the room, his gaze returning to the bar. There wasn't a bottle or glass behind it. Was Webster a teetotaler? He didn't have time to speculate. Ten minutes at the outside if Webster was going to look at a horse.

With speedy but precise movements, Pacer searched the room again. Damn! There was nothing.

In desperation he pushed the library ladder along the wall and began going through the books, concentrating on those that didn't look as though they'd had much use.

He was on the long wall opposite the door to the hall when he heard a swishing sound, like air escaping from somewhere. Caught at the top of the ladder with no time to jump and hide, he curled his body into a crouch.

When a section of bookshelf on one side of him started to move inward, he inched the well-oiled ladder backward, ready to spring on the person coming through the secret door.

The redhead walking into the study stopped him. It took all his stamina to stem the leap he'd been prepared to make. "Colm! Dammit, where did you come from?"

"And a happy hello to you." She looked up at him. "I came to fight at your side."

The funny, antiquated declaration stunned and moved him as nothing had ever done. "Stop that."

"What?"

"Making me think of loving you. I need all my concentration to be on Webster. Where are Dev and Con?"

"Around here somewhere with some men. They told me to wait at Rance's . . ."

"And you decided to disagree with that."

"They didn't listen to me about the passage, so I decided to see if I could get through. It hasn't been used in years."

Pacer's mind painted colorful pictures of her being buried or trapped in a tunnel with no one knowing where she was.

Jumping down from the ladder, he pulled her into his arms and kissed her fiercely. "Dammit, Colm, you could have been hurt, or worse." He closed his eyes for a second. "I can't lose you."

"Actually, I was pretty safe. Manuela, the housekeeper, is the only one who knows about the tunnel. She and a few members of her family keep it in working order. And she would never tell Milo Webster about it. She didn't even tell my father, because he wasn't a Fitzroy." Colm grinned, then touched Pacer's face. He was with her! He was safe! "No one would ever guess about the tunnel unless they were told. In fact, no one who belongs at Boru could be discovered on this land by outsiders unless they chose to be." She gazed around the study. "My mother kept this room for herself . . . and it was supposed to be mine, but my father used it."

Pacer shook his head. "It must have been difficult to have been at sword's point with your father all the time."

"Actually, after a time it was quite easy."

He hated the acid in her voice and hugged her. "We have to hurry."

"What were you doing?"

"I'm trying to go through the books, hoping they might hold a few secrets."

"Try the safe."

"There's nothing behind the picture."

"The safe is in the bar. Let me show you."

He shot a quick look at the door and followed her to the oak bar. She pushed a corner of it, and the carved center panel slid forward like a drawer.

Pacer glanced at the contents, then grabbed a plastic-wrapped packet shoved into the back corner.

"Nothing else?" Colm asked as he reached over her shoulder and shut the drawer.

"Let's hurry. We'll look at these in the tunnel. Is there air in there?"

She nodded as she walked back to the bookcase. Pressing a wooden rose in the wainscoting, she said, "Even this has to be turned and pressed a certain way."

"Hurry." Pacer had picked up the sound of voices, though they barely penetrated the heavy oak front door.

Colm stepped through the opening with Pacer right behind her. As soon as he was inside she pressed a switch and the door shut silently and swiftly. "I think Manuela and her family are planning a little uprising here if I don't gain back Boru legally and soon." Colm pointed to a small arsenal of weapons stashed in a corner.

Pacer looked around at the concrete wall and ceiling lights. "Very neatly done." His voice was barely a whisper.

"You can shout if you like, you can't be heard in the study. But . . ." She pressed a button on the wall. "We can hear them."

He nodded. "Let me know if they say anything interesting." Propping himself against the wall, he looked through the papers in the packet.

For several minutes Colm listened to Webster's and Brice's scathing denunciations of Dev and Con, then she became aware of Pacer's stillness. "What is it?"

His head came up sharply. "This is not what I was hoping to find . . . but it's very interesting." He held up a sheaf of papers that were wrinkled and yellowed. "This is the deed to the ranch. It's in your mother's name and there's no record of sale with it."

"What are you saying?" Colm's breathing was constricted, her heart thudding in a strange slow way. Hope curled inside her.

"I'm saying that unless Milo Webster doesn't know about the hidden safe and this deed, or he somehow hornswoggled your father into thinking there was a sale, then he's living here illegally. The ranch belongs to you."

Colm blinked. "And you think my father might not have known this?" She shook her head. "I hope he didn't. Though my father was a very sharp man where money was concerned. He kept track of every dime."

"I don't know what happened . . . but it looks as though you legally own Boru."

"I've always known my father couldn't have sold it . . . but I had no proof."

"Now you do." Pacer handed her the packet. "There are a few other things you might like to look at." He looked around him. "This is very well built."

Colm looked up from her perusal of the deed. "Yes. My great-grandfather Caleb had it built for protection during Indian attacks when he was a young man. The Indians never gave him any trouble, but since he did a little business with assorted smugglers in Galveston, the tunnel came in very handy for that." She smiled. "He bought smuggled cognac and rum, traded them for land." She looked up at the ceiling. "The original house was burned by disenchanted dealers, so the story goes. But the tunnel stayed because it was dirt then. When the house was rebuilt, this was all reinforced and strengthened."

Pacer leaned forward and kissed her nose. "You're

a beautiful lady, and I'm glad you have the firepower to get your ranch back."

"Because of you." Impulsively she reached up and cupped his chin in her hand, bringing his mouth to hers.

He slid both arms around her. "I love you . . . and I know it's a damn fool time to tell you."

She laughed, her eyes moist. "Sounds good, though." His crooked smile touched her like another caress.

"Yes." He kept his arms around her but glanced at his watch. "I thought I'd find out more about Webster in some of these papers, but maybe Dev and Con will be—"

"Shh, listen. That's my Uncle Henry."

Henry Bellin Troy's voice came through to Colm and Pacer in the tunnel. He was not trying to mask his dislike of Milo Webster. "Accept my offer. This place is no good for you. You've let the land go, the cattle herd is shot. There are other places."

"And why do you want Boru, Troy?"

"I want to give it to my niece as a gift. After all, it is rightfully hers. Her mother would want it that way."

"And you were always mooning around Vince's old lady, weren't you? He told me that."

"Watch your mouth."

"Hadn't you better watch yours? Brice is liable to take offense and throw you outta here."

"He can try."

Colm plucked at Pacer's sleeve. "Uncle Henry is so angry. I can hear it in his voice, but he's no match for them."

"Don't worry, darlin', I'll get in there if I have to." Pacer's few doubts about Henry Troy's loyalty to Colm were fading fast. He'd begun by being suspicious of everyone around Colm. But from what he could hear, Troy was not Colm's enemy.

The conversation in the study came to an abrupt end.

Colm stiffened. "What's going on? That sounded like shots."

"It's begun," Pacer said.

"They're leaving the study," she said, listening intently. "On the run, it sounds like."

"Let's go. Grab one of those." Pacer pointed to the revolvers wrapped in plastic. "I assume you can shoot."

"I'm a Texan. I can take a flea off a squirrel's ear." She hefted the gun and checked for ammunition. Then she looked up at Pacer. "But I'm not much of a hunter. I'd kill only if I needed food."

He touched her cheek. "I don't like shooting at people, either. Maybe we won't have to. You're beautiful, darlin'. Follow me close." At his nod she activated the opening and they stepped into the study.

"Hell," Pacer muttered, strolling to the window. "It sounds like Nam out there."

Colm followed him. Gunshots exploded rapidly, and she caught glimpses of men crouched behind Jeeps, trucks, trees. Occasionally one would sprint across the dusty ground and bullets would follow his path. She clutched Pacer's arm, not quite sure she believed what was happening. An old West shoot-out at Boru? She caught a glimpse of a dark-haired man racing from behind a truck, then diving behind an outcropping of rocks. Dev! Her grip tightened on Pacer's arm. What if his friends got hurt? What if Webster and his men won?

"Easy, darlin'," Pacer said. "It'll be all right. Dev

and Con are an army by themselves . . . and dangerous as hell when they're roused." His smile was twisted. "Be sorry for anyone who gets in their way."

"That's what they say about you."

He looked at her. "Yes. I've been known to cause trouble, but not to you, my love. Never to you." He kissed her quickly. "Wait here. I want to make sure Webster doesn't have any escape routes."

She opened her mouth to argue, then nodded acquiescence. After he left she remained by the window, watching and praying, flinching with fear every time she heard a man cry out, wounded by a bullet. It was a hellishly long wait for Pacer. When he returned she threw herself into his arms.

"Everything's fine, darlin'. Trust me."

"I do."

A shot came through the window and Pacer pulled her down to the floor, his body cushioning hers. "Boys are gettin' rough."

"We should help."

"We aren't getting in the way. They'll appreciate that." He kissed her, savoring her mouth. "I like it here on the floor with you."

The door burst open and Dev Abrams stood there.

"Smoking gun and all?" Pacer drawled, lifting Colm to her feet. "You're quite a picture."

Dev grinned. "It was a crap shoot and they crapped out." He glanced at Colm and shook his head. "How'd you get in here?"

"It's a long story," Pacer said. "My lady is determined."

"I have one like that," Dev said. "Caleb's with us. That man is one good shot."

"He and Uncle Henry taught me," Colm said faintly, not certain she believed it was over.

They heard a clatter in the hall and Dev smiled rakishly.

"We have some trash."

Lazarus and a few men ushered Webster and Brice into the room.

"How the hell did you get in here?" Webster asked, glaring at Pacer and Colm. His face was smudged with dirt.

"Watch how you talk to my lady in her own house," Pacer said sweetly.

Colm looked at him alarmed.

"Why's he so mad?" Con asked, striding into the room.

"I dunno," Dev said, his narrowed gaze on Pacer. "I hope nobody hurt his lady. I'm not into committing mass murder . . . unless we have to."

"You're going to prison, Webster," Pacer said.

"You're the one who'll be arrested, Dillon. You're trespassing on—"

"This isn't your land, Webster, and we have the deed to prove it. There's no bill of sale to you—and since the legal owner wouldn't have sold to you anyway, a bill of sale would have been illegal."

Webster couldn't stem the shudder that ran through him. He'd never seen a smile like that. The wrong end of a rattler.

"This land was given to me by my friend Vince Collamer."

"He couldn't have given it to anyone. This house and land were never his."

"That's a lie."

Dev leaned forward and pinched Webster's lips

together. "Don't say that to Mr. Dillon. It makes me angry."

Henry Troy pushed his way through the men, his anxious gaze finding Colm. "My dear girl, are you all right? When did you get here?"

"Mr. Troy isn't a bad shot either," Dev murmured.

"I'm all right, Uncle Henry. I'm with Pacer." Colm smiled shakily.

Henry looked from Colm to Pacer, then nodded slowly, a smile widening on his face.

"I still have some questions," Colm said, looking up at Pacer.

"Never mind, love. Things will get settled."

He moved away to shake his friends' hands, not taking his gaze from Colm. "She's beautiful, and brave as hell," he said to Dev and Con.

"But you're worried about something."

"You could always read me, Dev."

"What is it?" Con asked, studying his friend.

"Something happened to her when she was young. I want to know more about it."

"Oh? Something we can do?"

"I think so. I want you to find someone for me."

Eight

Driving through the gates of the senior Wendel's Long Island estate, Pacer was reminded of when he, Dev, and Con had spent their summer breaks from Princeton there. Mr. Wendel had seen to it that they worked hard taking care of the massive English-style garden, repairing the stone terrace, anything that needed to be done. What had been their boss's name? Big Bill Marsden, but the three of them had called him sir.

His two friends were already at the palatial mansion. Pacer could hear their voices as he walked down the hall to the study. He pushed open the door and looked from one to the other.

"This is Kelso?" he asked, turning his gaze to the bull-faced man sitting there.

"Who's he, Mr. Abrams?" the man said. "I thought I was being interviewed for a job."

"And you might get a job, Tweedy." Dev spoke in a low, even tone to the now uneasy man.

"We didn't get Kelso, Pace," Con said. "Apparently this man was his best friend in Folsom."

"We want to know about Kelso," Pacer said, raising his voice to get Tweedy's attention. He didn't waste time on amenities. "If you tell the truth, we'll arrange for a job tryout for you. If you lie, you'll get the hell out of here, fast. There will be no job and no hope of getting one."

"Kelso? He's been dead a couple a' years now."

Pacer exhaled heavily.

"You were his best friend," Dev said. "The word is he told you everything. Right?"

Tweedy looked from one to the other. "Mebbe."

"Get out," Pacer said. "Forget the job. Give him a few bucks." Pacer strode to the door.

"Wait, wait. Whattaya wanta know?"

Pacer stopped and turned. "About the time Kelso was arrested for assaulting a young girl on the Fitzroy ranch in Texas." Pacer watched Tweedy's piggy eyes blink as his mind turned over the information he had.

"Yeah, that was Collamer's kid, but it fizzled. Some dude caught Petey, shot him. . . ."

"Troy," Dev murmured.

Tweedy shook his head. "Petey wanted to get Collamer for that. Said he would, too, but he was doing big time by then." Tweedy stared at the whiskey decanter, licking his dry lips. "Could use a drink."

"That can wait." Pacer's blood had congealed in his veins. Anger was pumping through him. His friends' tight faces told him they were tuned into his wave length. "Explain."

"Whattaya mean? I told ya. Old man Collamer set it up for Petey to have a go at his kid. Said he needed to teach her a lesson. Wish it had been me, I'da—"

Dev threw himself at Pacer. "Con, get him out of here! I can't hold Pace." Dev could feel himself being pushed inexorably backward. "And lock the door. Fly him out of here now." Pacer was going to kill Tweedy. There was no doubt in Dev's mind. "Dammit, Pace, you're crushing me." Dev had been backed against the desk.

"Sorry." Inhaling slowly, thinking of Colm, safe and at home, soothed him. But the fire of hate against Vince Collamer didn't flag.

"I'm glad Collamer's dead," Dev said. "Otherwise we would have to kill him. I don't think Felicity wants me to go to jail." Dev exhaled when Pacer's face cracked a slight smile.

"Yeah, she went through that once, and it wasn't good." Pacer's hand shook when he put it up to his face. "Damn his soul."

"Yeah. Con'll take care of everything with Tweedy and he and I will handle things here. You can get a flight out of here to Houston. I'll call for you."

"Thanks." Pacer stared at his friend. "She suffered and she still does. Damn, damn, damn."

"Get going, chum. You'll come up with the right words to deal with this."

"I have to."

Dev winced at the look of torture in his friend's eyes. "You think she knew her father did this to her?"

"I think subconsciously she knows."

"Damn. I would have enjoyed killing Vince Collamer."

Not an hour later Pacer was in the air on his way to Houston. He refused all food and drink, then closed his eyes and forced himself into the trance that his Indian grandfather had taught him. To rest, to close off the world, let the soul and mind heal, drift away from earth, away from the evil that man created.

Houston International was a madhouse, but he saw her at once. "What are you doing here?" he asked as he hugged her.

"Con called me and said you'd be on this flight. Do you suppose he knew how much I missed you?"

"Or how much I missed you." He leaned down and kissed her hard. "Let's go." Pacer could feel her concern, her quick glances, but he hurried her through the airport to the parking lot.

Once behind the wheel in her car he turned to Colm and took her in his arms, kissing her thoroughly, savoring her touch. "That's better."

Now was the time to tell her, he thought, while they were driving home. He had no intention of going to the apartment or to Fitzroy's. The ranch was a haven to her—and the scene of the crime. Damn! He drew in an unsteady breath.

"Tell me what it is, Pacer. I know something's terribly wrong."

"Now you're acting like both my grandmothers."

"Don't slough it off. You can't. I've begun to know you, Pacer Creekwood Dillon."

"Do you trust me?"

"With all that's in me."

"Good. You'll know everything I do, darlin'."

He reached across the seat of the Mercedes and pulled her close to him. "That's the one thing I like about bench seats."

"Silly man." Fear fluttered through her. Never once

since they'd met had Pacer been evasive, but he was now.

What had happened in New York? she wondered. Who had he seen? Who had gotten past his guard and shaken the unflappable Pacer Creekwood Dillon? Or was he tired of her so soon? Had he stopped loving her? Nonsense. He loved her and she knew that.

"I'll tell you all about it when we get home, love," he said. The vibrations coming off her thick and fast telegraphed her uncertainties, her questions.

Love! she thought. He called her love. Pacer wouldn't do that unless he meant it. Relief flooded her. Nothing was more important than that. Sometimes it seemed like a dream that she could have the happiness that Pacer offered. She needed his love, wanted him so much. He pushed the darkness away.

He took her hand and lifted it to his mouth. "The wedding is upon us, love. Are you ready?"

"Very ready. Are you?"

"I can't wait to make you Colm Fitzroy Dillon." He glanced at her and saw the shadow in her smile. He would make the shadows disappear.

Colm sat up straight and took note of their direction. "You're going to the ranch."

"Yes, my darling, I am."

Now he'd called her "darling" not "darlin'." His voice was clipped, taut. Though he was gentle with her, there was a tension in him. "You're making me nervous."

"Don't be. Everything's fine. I just need to talk to you alone."

"All right."

She let her head fall to his shoulder. She loved

him, she needed him. Emptying her mind of everything but that, she stared out the windshield.

Sleep overtook her like a black cloak.

"I'm glad you're sleeping, my angel," Pacer whispered. "You'll need your strength when I tell you this."

All during the flight to Houston he'd wrestled with the idea of not telling her what Tweedy had told him. The rest of the investigation into Petey Kelso had affirmed that he'd been a man of few principles. But he was an angel compared with the man who'd thrown his child to the wolves, arranged her rape, risked her life and her sanity. Thank God Henry Troy had intervened.

Pacer stopped the car in the courtyard, then got out and went around to the passenger side. He lifted Colm into his arms without waking her.

Manuela opened the door and gazed at Colm with concern as he carried her inside.

"It's all right," he said. "The señorita is just drowsy. I'm taking her into the study."

"I will bring fresh lemonade, Señor Pacer."

"Thank you."

Colm woke when he laid her on the couch. "Are we home?"

He chuckled. "Yes." He knew exactly what she meant. "Home" would always be the ranch.

"Tell me." Struggling to sit up she stared up at him.

"Manuela is bringing us a cold drink. Then I will." He turned as the door behind him opened and the housekeeper entered with a tray.

Colm was on edge. For the first time in memory

she was impatient with Manuela's precise ways. Finally the woman was gone.

"Well?" Colm asked impatiently.

"First of all, let me say that I'd rather not tell you, but I've promised to be up front with you, not keep things from you." Pacer looked down at her, then knelt before her. "I love you and I will always tell you the truth."

"Thank you." Shivers of fear rode her. Her hands shook and her breath came in short bursts. The adrenaline pumping through her was an alien poison, not a stimulus. "Go on."

Pacer didn't miss the tremor in her voice. "When you told me about the time you were assaulted and about your Uncle Henry saving you, I got curious."

"Because you wondered that a young girl from a wealthy family would not be protected against such things."

"Yes."

"And what did you find?" She didn't want to hear. She had to fight not to cover her ears.

"That the man who assaulted you is dead."

"And?"

"And that your father paid the man to accost you." He felt her body shake and admired her courage. But maybe, he thought, tears and hysterics would have been better.

Tight bands that had manacled her being for so long let go. Relief, anger, pity coursed through her. "I—I think I've always known that. I know Uncle Henry and Rance were fiercely protective after that. They seemed to show up whenever I was home. And whatever Uncle Henry said to my father bothered him a great deal. Shortly afterward I was sent to boarding school. I was lonely, but glad to be away from home. I hated to return even at holidays." Colm leaned forward until her head rested against Pacer's shoulder.

"What are you thinking?" he asked, worried that the shock had been too great. Maybe he shouldn't have told her. Damn. Nothing should hurt her, and nothing was going to if he could help it.

She took a deep breath. "I was always so relieved when Uncle Henry would call and tell me he was taking me on ski trips or vacations when I was home from school. Sometimes Rance would take me on camping trips. But mostly it was Uncle Henry. Summers I went to camp."

"So, that's why Henry and Rance are so protective of you." Something in the back of Pacer's mind was clamoring to get out, but it didn't happen. Whatever it was stayed locked in his mind. Why did a bell go off in his head every time Henry Bellin Troy's name was mentioned?

"What are *you* thinking?" Colm asked. She threaded her fingers through his hair, loving the feel of it. Hearing about her father's evil actions was anticlimactic and not a surprise. A numbness had taken hold of her. She felt detached from everything except Pacer.

"Something's bugging me," he said, "but I can't get a handle on it." He poured her some lemonade and handed her the glass.

She drank some, then rose to her feet, pacing the beloved study. The mahogany wall panels had been hand-crafted in Ireland and shipped over. Looking up at the painting of her mother over the mantel, Colm sighed. "I wish my mother had lived longer.

There was so much I needed to know. But then she was always so secretive, just like the rest of the Fitzroys."

"What do you mean, darlin'? How do you know that about her?"

Colm smiled. "She left me letters and notes, all of them very cryptic." She stared at the painting. "I've always felt there was a message there, but I've never found it."

Pacer followed her glance to the painting. "The messages were in the painting?"

"That's the way it sounded to me when I read the letters, but there's nothing. Perhaps I'll get some experts to examine the painting one day."

"Did your father ever see the letters she left for you?"

"No. They were given to me by Uncle Henry. Mother gave them to him for safekeeping."

"I see."

"Along with the numbered bank accounts in Switzerland belonging to Fitzroy's. My father suspected something like that, but he was never able to discover anything concrete." Colm's smile was twisted. "I didn't know any of this until after he died."

"But you wouldn't have told him if you had known."

"Certainly not. Those monies buttressed the company after my father's death when we realized how he'd bled Fitzroy's."

"Tell me about the painting."

"Nothing to tell." She shrugged, remembering her disappointment and chagrin when she hadn't discovered anything upon examining the painting. "It was done by a renowned French portraitist whose work was well respected. And it was one of the frustrations of my father's life. He tried to sell it once, but it can't be removed without taking down the wall. The frame is part of the structure and the canvas is cemented to the frame."

Pacer whistled, rising to his feet. "That's a damned stupid thing to do to something so valuable. Unless . . ." He touched Colm's arm. "I don't suppose you have the cryptic letters your mother left."

"Of course I do." She walked to the bar and opened the safe. "When you got the ranch back for me I transferred many of my personal things out here." She removed a case and took a small bundle of papers from it. "These are my mother's letters to me. She wrote them when she was dying, I assume. Many of them are sad." She spread them out on the coffee table, then handed one to Pacer. "This was the letter Uncle Henry gave me right after my mother died."

Pacer read.

The painting in the library has my words for you, darling. The truth is written there. My love is with you always. Mother.

He walked over to the sliding ladder, unhooked it from its railing, and carried it over to the mantel.

"It's a waste of time, Pacer. I've been up there many times. There's no writing in any language."

"Then I won't look at the painting. I'll look at the frame, darlin'." Something pulled him to the painting. Was it Adaira herself? His body tingled with an awareness he'd often felt in Nam.

Colm moved closer, fascinated by the way his hands ran over the ornately carved wood. "My father was convinced he could get good money for the frame, but everyone said it was too tied into the structure to attempt its removal."

"Ummm." The rosettes carved into the wide wooden frame were delicate and beautifully done—except for one. He pressed it. There was an unmistakable click. Pacer moved or the swinging painting would have struck him, the oiled hinges making no sound. "Another tunnel of sorts in the labyrinth."

Colm gasped. "I never knew it was there." She laughed out loud. "Again my mother and grandfather thwarted my father." Dragging over a straightbacked chair she climbed onto it.

"Get down, Colm. I'll check this out for you."

"Well, hurry then!"

He smiled down at her. "What's the rush? The contents have been here quite a while by the look of it."

"I want to see." Something of her mother's, a message, a remembrance. Colm was impatient. Her lovely mother, whom she barely remembered, had remembered her.

Pacer picked up envelopes, deeds, papers, some letters. These he lowered to her. One small packet of oilcloth had Colm's name inscribed on the satin ribbon that held it closed.

Colm studied the deeds, the many bearer bonds clustered among the legal papers. "Pacer, look at the land we own. My family seemed to have made very sure that my father wouldn't get his hands on these holdings." Pain fluttered through her. "Why did she ever marry him, Pacer? She couldn't have loved him. Otherwise, why would she have hidden so many things from him?"

"Maybe she loved him at first but then discovered she couldn't trust him to care for her legacy."

"I don't think you believe that. I know I don't."

Pacer got down from the ladder and sat beside her on the sofa. "I can't dislike a man who fathered you, no matter what my instincts tell me."

She patted his cheek, kissing him gently. "But you didn't trust Vince Collamer, did you?"

He shook his head. "I thought he played too close to the edge for ethics and principle . . . but there are many men who do the same who are considered pillars of their communities."

"Ummm, maybe so." Colm only scanned many of the papers. There was time for her and Pacer to read them at their leisure. Doing anything with Pacer was exciting and wonderful. Lifting a scroll-like paper, she shook her head in wonder. "I'm sure my father never knew about any of these things. I didn't. Orange groves, oil wells, rural and city properties. Oh, my goodness, this piece of land is prime downtown Houston real estate." She looked up grinning, but her smile faded when she noticed he hadn't heard her. "What is it?"

"That cryptic note about the painting holding the information you need might be this, darlin'." He put the oilcloth-wrapped package in her lap. "Your name is on this one."

"Open it, please," she said breathily.

"All right." He noted that his own hands were shaking a bit. Right now he and Colm were close, happy. It made the bile rise in him to think of her reading anything that could hurt her. "This is a birth certificate stating that you were born to Adaira

Marie Fitzroy and Vincent Collamer. Your baptized name was Colm Fitzroy Collamer."

"I changed it to Fitzroy when I came of age."

"I know." He sifted through the letters, quickly reading the notations. "More advisement on holdings that you should see." The last was an envelope which said COLM FITZROY COLLAMER, FOR YOUR EYES ONLY. "Read it, darlin'."

"No, you do it. I don't think I can." Strange sensations prickled through her. She felt hot, suffocated in the air-conditioned room, as though someone else were there, close to her. Mother?

Threading her hands together she watched Pacer slit the envelope. She wanted and didn't want to know what it said. "Be careful."

"I will." Her nervousness communicated itself to him. Damn the world to hell if she was hurt again. Lifting out a rather thick letter, he opened it. Despite the good condition of the paper, he was careful. He read aloud the date on the letter.

"That was just before my mother died." Grief lanced through her. "I—I didn't really know her, but I loved her."

"I know."

"Read it."

"All right."

My Darling Child,

I will always love you in this world and the next. I have to put the truth down on paper now because I fear for my safety. With your grandfather gone, Vince is getting more demanding. He knows that much of what belongs to the Fitzroys is kept from him, both physically and legally. It is the only way to insure your legacy.

Never doubt that Vince Collamer is dangerous. I swear to you I didn't know that when I married him, or I never would have put you and myself in harm's way.

Pacer stopped reading when Colm gripped his hand. "Easy, darlin'."

"What does she mean?"

"I'm not sure. Shall I continue?" If Collamer had killed Colm's mother, he'd exhume his damn body and put the remains in quicklime. "Darlin'?"

"Read, Pacer. I'm glad you're with me."

"I'll always be at your side."

You must forgive me for a deception that I felt necessary. Only your grandfather knew about this, and now so do you.

Your father is not Vincent Collamer. I was never in love with him. I married him in desperation because the man I loved, your father, was married. To prevent shame and friction, I agreed to marry Vince even though I knew he wanted me only for my money and property. Our married years haven't been happy, and to add to the bitterness, the man I loved lost his wife shortly before you were born. I could have married him had I waited, but I didn't know that.

Soon after I married Vince, I began to fear him so much that I never told him that you weren't his. He is a small, mean man who wouldn't have been any kinder to a child than he was to me, especially a child who wasn't his. . . .

Pacer paused, seeing Colm's tears, hearing her sobs. "Darlin', don't. . . ."

"I'm happy, so happy. I never felt he was my father. I hated him and felt so guilty for that. Now I'm free." Pressing her hand against her middle, she sighed. "I think I always knew he couldn't be my father."

Pacer put his arm around her shoulders and hugged her. "Nothing will ever hurt you again like he did. I wouldn't let it. I love you, my Colm."

"Pacer, I love you so much. I wonder if you can ever understand how much. You gave me life." Her eyes widened. "Who is my father?"

"Wait, there's more."

So, my darling girl, now you know.
I loved your father, and love him now as he loved me and loves me yet. We were desperate for each other, but his wife was very ill and I couldn't let him make such a painful choice. So he never knew that he had a wonderful child like you. Your smile is so like his—

"Pacer, what is it?"

"I think I know who your father is, darlin'." He grinned at her. "And you'll be pleased." Relief coursed through him like a flood. Standing abruptly, he pulled her up, lifting her off her feet, and whirled her around and around.

"Who? Who?" she asked.

"You sound like an owl." Pacer laughed out loud

for the sheer joy of knowing that Colm would be so happy. "Your mother was right. Your smile is like his. I noticed something familiar the first time I met him, but didn't connect it until now." Still holding her above the floor, he kissed her soundly.

"Pacer Creekwood Dillon! How can you keep me dangling like this?"

"Figuratively or literally?"

"Stop!"

"I'm just happy for you."

"Pacer!"

"Kiss me."

"Tell me."

He set her down, then sat on the sofa, pulling her onto his lap. "I'll read it to you . . . but I won't be surprised."

"Pacer, stop."

"All right."

Tell your father, because I know he loves you and you love him. Your real name should have been Colm Fitzroy Bellin Troy.

Pacer let the paper drop when Colm's hands tightened around his neck. "Happy?" he asked.

"Uncle Henry is my father?"

"Yes. When I met him I thought there was something familiar about him, but I couldn't pinpoint it. You both have the same smile."

"I do—we do," Colm said dazedly. Then she looked at Pacer. "What do you think about my new name?"

"I like it." He hesitated. "Would you like to use that instead of Dillon?"

She shook her head. "I'll just sandwich it in. . . ."

Maybe I shouldn't. I haven't asked him . . . I should. . . ."

"Henry will be overjoyed, darlin'. I would swear to it."

"I've always loved him."

"And he feels the same. The first time he met me and saw the way I was staring at you, he looked me over pretty carefully."

"Did he?" Colm was shaken. All the years of ambivalent feelings toward Vince Collamer, castigating herself because she wasn't loyal or loving enough to him, had been her subconscious response to the truth.

"Yes." Pacer inhaled deeply, loving the scent of her. "Will he give me the third degree, do you think?"

What would he do? she wondered. Uncle Henry was her father! It was all so unbelievable, so wonderful. She gazed at the man holding her.

"What are you thinking?" he asked.

"How my life has changed in so many ways since you came into it. How much I love you."

Her slow smile made his heart pound in his throat. "And you are very aware of how much power you have over me, Colm Fitzroy Bellin Troy."

"That's me." Nuzzling against him, she nipped his ear. "Oooh, I can feel your lap undergoing a change."

"Vixen."

"I didn't say I didn't like the change. I feel like celebrating."

"Great." Pacer couldn't get enough air into his lungs and there was a thrumming in his ears. "Do you want me to get the champagne?" The thought of letting her go was almost painful.

"No," she breathed into his ear. "I want you to remove my clothes and I'll take off yours. Then we'll dance and cavort and . . ." She let her tongue trace his ear, and he groaned.

"I will never have enough of you."

"Show me."

He surged to his feet, holding her. "I fully intend to do just that."

"Good. I didn't want to do all the work."

"Oh, lady, when we get to the bed, you won't have to work at all."

"I like it when your eyes turn pewter. That means you're really excited." Soon this wonderful man would be her husband. Dreams did come true. He encompassed it all for her—love, passion, cherishing.

"Then they must have been pewter-colored since I met you. I've been aroused from moment one."

Nine

The day of the wedding dawned bright and beautiful. Texas put on her best face.

Colm looked out the window of the bedroom that had been her mother's and grandfather's on Boru. It belonged to her, and soon to Pacer as well . . . and someday to their children.

He had done so much for her. And in a few hours she would be his wife. Happiness flooded through her.

Her own father would be giving her away in marriage, as well as Rance. Her body flushed with joy as she recalled Henry Troy's delight when she had told him she was his daughter.

"You're so like Adaira, Colm," he'd said, and she had seen the flash of pain in his eyes. "I still miss her—but now I have you. I should have known you were mine, my darling child. I've always loved you as though you were."

"I think I must have always known too, Father."
Calling him father for the first time had been ecstasy.

Henry's face had hardened. "From what you and
Pacer have told me about Vince Collamer, it doesn't
surprise me that the police are now sure his death
was no accident. Not that Milo Webster would ever
admit to it. But someone was bound to have killed
Collamer. I would have myself if I'd known what he'd
planned for you."

"Pacer says he was a pathetic man, one-dimensional,
thin as paper. I feel no animosity now, Father, just
relief." When Henry had hugged her, she embraced
him back. "I have my own father. How can I hate
Vince Collamer or anyone else?"

Henry had pulled back from her. "He was a bastard. Pacer is convinced he would have had you
confined to a mental hospital after the assault."

"But you saved me from Petey Kelso, Father."

"I loved you so much that day. You were so brave
when I took you to the hospital, comforting me when
I assured you my anger wasn't directed at you." He
had hugged her once more. "I've found my Adaira
again in you, child."

"I'm glad you'll be living on the ranch soon, Father, and that you like the place Pacer is having
built for you."

"He couldn't have given me a nicer gift."

"He thought we might want to be near each other."

Now it was her wedding day. Colm's eyes moist-
ened when she thought of her father and the wonderful man who would soon be her husband.

Pacer entered the bedroom, his breath catching in
his throat. Colm was a goddess in ivory lace and
silk. He paused, realizing that she was smiling into

the mirror, but the vision she studied was in her mind.

He hadn't knocked, because the door was ajar. He savored the moment when he could just gaze at her. She was breathtaking in her wedding gown. The off-the-shoulder design revealed skin just as silky as the dress. "You're a princess."

Startled, Colm turned quickly, the delicate fabric swirling and rustling around her. "You're beautiful, Pacer Creekwood Dillon." His handmade black silk suit emphasized the silvery streaks in his hair, and his Gucci shoes in softest leather were black and sleek. "But you're not supposed to see the bride until the ceremony."

"I missed you."

"Me too." Love pulsed through her. She reached out to him.

"You're too beautiful to kiss."

"Never that."

He bent to her mouth. "You were daydreaming when I came in, darlin'."

"About my father and you."

She tasted like honey, and the scent of her skin was like dew-wet flowers. "My wife."

"Not yet."

"Always my wife."

Heat fanned between her legs as it had done since the first time he'd touched her, the moistness there an excitement in itself.

"*Madre de Dios!* What are you doing here, señor? It is not for you to see your bride yet." Manuela glowered at them, arms akimbo. "Out of here."

"I'll see you soon." Pacer's kiss blistered her mouth.

Colm reluctantly opened her eyes after he'd gone.

"*Mucho hombre,*" the housekeeper muttered, her glance going over Colm. "He loves you."

"Yes."

"Be happy with him . . . and with your father." Manuela's face softened. "That would make your *mamacita* very happy too."

"Thank you."

"It is time."

As she descended the stairs, Colm looked right into the eyes of Rance and then her father. She felt calm, serene. There were still some unknowns between Pacer and herself, but they would take care of themselves. Love was clear between them, life was sweet to ponder. Everything else was extraneous, not that important.

Marrying Pacer would bring her life into focus.

Her two attendants waiting at the entrance to the spacious living room smiled at each other as a violin and harp played Mendelssohn.

Felicity leaned toward Heller. "This makes me more nervous than my own wedding did."

"You look great, so do our men. But Pacer and Colm are awesome."

The two women turned to watch the bride enter on the arms of her father and Rance.

Pacer couldn't take his eyes off her. He'd been totally committed to her at first sight. Now she would be his.

The vows were spoken in the ancient rite, the covenant echoing up into the stucco ceilings, vibrating through the small gathering.

"I, Pacer, take thee, Colm . . ."

"I, Colm, take thee, Pacer . . ."

"You may kiss the bride." The Franciscan priest gave them his blessing.

"Open your eyes, wife. It's over."

"Are you mine?"

The ingenuous question was acknowledged by a river of titters that rippled around the room.

"You know I am."

"She's our aunt now, isn't she, Simeon?"

The rest of the progeny of the Wendel and Abrams clans looked to the oldest for confirmation. His staid nod made the grins burst through, the solemnity over.

"Let the games begin," Dev said mildly, kissing his wife behind the ear.

"Devil." Felicity stroked his cheek as she often did. It still seemed a miracle to her that they were together. Her gaze wandered to Con and Heller who were holding hands. "We're very lucky, Dev."

"We are, my love, we are." Dev glanced at the newlyweds. They had eyes only for each other.

"Let's get out of here," Pacer whispered urgently to Colm.

"So soon? Wouldn't that be impolite?" Still, she was desperate to be alone with her new husband.

"I don't care about politeness. I want to be alone with you. Now."

"Sounds wonderful." She grinned. "All right, let's leave."

They made their good-byes in record time, and Colm pretended not to notice the grins on Dev's and Con's faces.

Pacer flew the Fitzroy helicopter to Galveston. They had little to say on the flight. The enormity of what she had done was just hitting Colm. She who had said she would never marry was now Pacer Creekwood Dillon's wife. He had walked into her life only a couple of months ago and had turned it topsy-turvy. But she loved him so much. She glanced at him, certain now that marrying him was the best thing she had ever done.

They landed at the helipad in Galveston within sight of the marina and boarded a motorized launch that took them to the yacht Pacer had chartered for their honeymoon cruise.

Pacer signaled to the captain to get under way, then guided Colm down to the main cabins. "In here, darlin'," he said, opening the door to their stateroom.

"It's beautiful, Pacer," she said, gazing around at the polished wood walls and gleaming brass fixtures.

"As you are," he murmured, and began unbuttoning the long row of pearl buttons down her back. He slid the dress off her, then the long slip, and stepped back. Then he closed his eyes. Dressed only in high heels, stockings, and a silky teddy, Colm was the most exciting woman he'd ever seen. "I shouldn't do this to myself . . . but it's wonderful."

She smiled. "Suffering, are you?"

"Erotic agony, darlin'." He carelessly stripped off his own clothes, then lifted her up and carried her to the king-size bed. The thought of making love to her with those high heels on made the blood thunder through his veins. He sat on the edge of the bed, holding her in his lap. When she gazed up at him, he saw a hint of a shadow in her eyes. "What is it?" he asked.

She ducked her head. "It isn't important."

"Everything about you is important. Tell me."

She took a deep breath. "You haven't told me about the phone call from that FBI agent the other night."

His arms tightened around her. "I'm sorry, but he didn't have much to say. Their preliminary investigation reveals that Milo Webster scammed the ranch from Vince Collamer, and that he probably had Collamer killed." Pacer shrugged. "Since Webster will never confess to anything, it might take time proving it . . . but prove it we will. I've made up my mind to that. Webster is going to pay for it all."

Pacer's lazy smile sent shivers through her. "And you have the patience to see it through."

"Yes." He kissed her hands. "Does that bother you?"

"No. I don't feel vengeful, but I don't want to see him out of prison until he's paid his debt either."

"That's my girl."

She shook her head. "The whole mess is incredible."

Pacer's face tightened. "It was Stefan Denys who tried to run you down in the garage, and he and his chum were the ones who broke into your apartment." His eyes narrowed. "The FBI agent seemed to think that Brice will crack and we'll learn what they were after."

Colm touched her mouth to the corner of his. "Thank you, husband, for all you've done for me . . . and my mother."

"You're most welcome, wife. Pleasing you brings me pleasure." To him she was like the sweetest peach, and he wanted badly to nibble on her. His whole being was filled with want for her. He brushed the silken tendrils from her forehead with his mouth. There would never be a time when he didn't want her.

"Your heart's beating very hard," she said, pressing one hand against his chest.

"I want you and love you."

Tears rose unbidden in her eyes and tumbled down her cheeks. "You make all good things happen, Pacer."

He couldn't lick the tears fast enough, but he tried.

Pushing him back so that they were lying on the bed, Colm rolled on top of him. "I love you and I'm feeling very sexy. How do you feel?"

"Totally disinterested," he said hoarsely, his hardening body racing toward explosion.

"Umm, totally disinterested feels good." She undulated gently. "Do you like it?"

"Too much." Wanting to be gentle, he tried to lift her down next to him.

"No. I want this." Reaching down she unsnapped her teddy and lowered herself onto him.

"God! Colm . . . baby." Pacer groaned as she began a sweet rhythm. "I can't—"

"Don't hold back. It's wonderful."

He reared up, filling her, loving her as she took him over the edge.

In sweet surrender she joined him in the ecstatic spiral that sent them out beyond the sun and moon.

"That was very, very good," she whispered, falling forward on his body.

It was better every time they loved, he thought. How could that happen? Colm was magic for him.

"Why are you smiling?" She brushed her fingers through his hair, noting the sheen of perspiration on his forehead.

"Because you're wonderful and because my Irish

grandmother would now consider me a success. I've managed to land a redheaded colleen."

"Land, did you say? Spalpeen! I'll get you for that."

His eyes snapped open. "That sounded wonderful. Did you ever live in Ireland?"

"I visited there. I liked it. I could live in Ireland."

"We could take long visits there."

She stroked his face. "You're remembering something, but not all the recollections are sweet. Tell me."

"You're right. I was remembering the sweet loving things my father would say to my mother. Though he'd been born in this country, he could mimic his Irish mother's way of talking." Pacer smiled. "They were always hugging and kissing, and he would whisper endearments in an Irish accent. Those were happy times in my life." He looked at her. "You brought happiness back into my life."

"As you did to mine."

"You're all things to me, Colm, love." He held her lightly, kissing her ring finger.

"Good." Never had she experienced such a rush of protectiveness. "I'll want to cherish you all my life, Pacer Creekwood Dillon." She leaned forward, forgetting that she was still, in essence, attached to her husband until he groaned. "Oh, did I hurt you?"

"No, baby, you didn't hurt me, but you are arousing me."

She chuckled. "That shouldn't surprise you."

"My grandmother would say you've the 'tooch.' "

"Is she still alive?"

"No, she died in Ireland many years ago, inordinately proud of her half-breed grandson."

"I can empathize with that. I feel the same way."

Wriggling gently, Colm grinned at his obvious reaction. "Ooo, I can feel that."

"So can I. I love you, lady, and I never thought I'd say that to a woman who owned me. I never, never imagined there could be a woman I would willingly give my life to until I met you."

"Shocking, to be sure. But only fair. You own me." She kissed him.

"What're you thinking, darlin'?"

"I think I'd like a baby right away."

Then Pacer's body jerked in surprise and he groaned again. "I forgot we were attached." He stared at her. "I'd like a baby too. Shall we cruise around the world and practice?"

"Even though we have a ranch and Fitzroy's to run?"

"No problem. We've got a fine staff." Pacer was fast losing control.

"There is that." Colm caught her breath when he raised his hips. "This is wonderful."

"I think we'll talk another time."

Pacer loved her body with his mouth.

Colm did the same to him.

"Darlin'!"

"It's my turn." Sucking gently on his nipples gave her a rippling delight that felt like a thousand sexy needles. All the feeling burning inside her, stifled in the loveless atmosphere created by Vince Collamer, now surfaced. It crashed through the barriers she'd erected to protect herself against a biting sarcasm, a nastiness calculated to break her down.

In an eruption of joy she loved the man who'd come into her life and had become her buffer, friend, and lover.

"You are one hot lover, wife." Pacer felt unfettered, released from the strictures he'd placed on his life. All the control that had taken years to mold and form had been blown apart by dynamite called Colm. "Wait!"

"Why?"

"Dunno." The world whirled around him because she caressed him most intimately. Shivering with love and delight, he pulled her up his body. "I will always need you."

"And I you." An erotic fever had her in its grip. "If I don't have you in five seconds I'll—I'll explode."

He gripped her gently, then entered her with a fierce sweetness that had her gasping. As the sounds of passion broke from her, his libido climbed. At the hoarse cry of his name on her lips, he spilled into her, loving her from a past of a thousand years and a millenium into the future.

They'd been back from their honeymoon for weeks, and the closeness had grown every day.

So, Pacer wondered, why did he feel, at this moment on this particular evening, that his new wife was holding back?

"You've been staring at me since we left the office," she said as they walked into the house at Boru.

"And all during the flight here." He had gotten into the habit of flying the helicopter out to the ranch in the middle of the week, flying back to Houston on Thursday morning, then returning on Friday afternoon so they could have weekends at the ranch.

She grinned. "Maybe it's just TGIF."

"Oh? Since when have you been so chary of work that you blessed Fridays." His gaze swept over her. She was different. Ebullient. Gleeful. "What have you done now behind my back? Not the bag-of-water-over-the-stable-door trick again?"

"Nooo, but you'll have to admit that was amusing."

He had thought so too, because he had been thoroughly charmed by her gales of laughter when the water had spilled over him. The ranch hands had been as delighted as he to watch their mistress caught up in irrepressible humor. But this was more than that. "Planning to snare me in a noose so that I'm hanging by my heels from the oak tree in the front of the house?"

"No, but it's an innovative idea for the future."

Her peals of laughter delighted and intrigued him. "You're happy, aren't you?"

Tears pricked her eyes at the awe in his voice. "What woman wouldn't be, married to you, Pacer, love?" She put her hand to her mouth and moved closer. "I'll give you three guesses."

"Okay." he scooped her into his arms and carried her easily, as he often did, up the stairs to their bedroom. They always changed into casual clothes for dining *à deux*. "Let's see—"

"I'm pregnant," she blurted. Her arms tightened around his neck when she felt him stagger on the stairs, but he caught himself quickly.

"No! Us? You and me? Wow, we're pretty good, aren't we?" Giddy, as though drunk with the power of it all, he hurried into their room. "Are you sure?"

"Yes. You know I'm never late. I'm almost three weeks."

He placed her on the bed and kneeled in front of

her, putting his face in her lap. "I love you. Are you well?"

"Yes, and I love you."

"I'll spend my life trying to show you how much you mean to me, but I don't know if it's possible." He lifted her hand and stroked her thumb over her wedding ring. Inscribed in turquoise on the gold were the Creek words that meant Beautiful Woman. "I need your warmth and light, Colm."

"And I'll always need you."

Embracing, they fell back on the bed to love and cherish each other.

The sun went down in the Texas sky, but the white heat of love sustained them and kept them safe.

THE EDITOR'S CORNER

What an extraordinary sextet of heroes we have for you next month! And the heroines are wonderful, too, but who's paying all that much attention when there are such fantastic men around?

Iris Johansen is back with a vibrantly emotional, truly thrilling romance, **MAGNIFICENT FOLLY**, LOVESWEPT #342. Iris's man of the month is Andrew Ramsey. (Remember him? Surprised to reencounter him as a hero? Well, he is a marvelous—no, magnificent—one!) When this handsome, unusually talented, and sensitive man appears in Lily Deslin's life, she almost goes into shock. The intuitive stranger attracts her wildly, while almost scaring her to death. Abruptly, Lily learns that Andrew has played a very special, very intimate role in her life and, having appeared as if by magic, is on the scene to protect her and her beloved daughter Cassie. Before the danger from the outside world begins, Lily is already in trouble because Andrew is unleashing in her powerful emotions and a deep secret she's kept buried for years. Iris's **GOLDEN CLASSIC, THE TRUSTWORTHY RED-HEAD,** is now on sale. If you read it—and we hope you will—we believe you'll have an especially wonderful time with **MAGNIFICENT FOLLY,** as Andrew, Lily, and Cassie take you back to Alex Ben Rashid's Sedikhan.

Ivan Rasmussen is one of the most gorgeous and dashing heroes ever . . . and you won't want to miss his love story in Janet Evanovich's **IVAN TAKES A WIFE,** LOVESWEPT #343. The fun begins when Stephanie Lowe substitutes for her cousin as cook on board Ivan's windjammer cruise in Maine coastal waters. Descended from a pirate, Ivan sweeps Stephanie off her feet while laughing at her Calamity Jane performance in his galley. He had never thought of settling down until he embraced Stephanie, and she had never been made to feel cherished until Ivan teased and flirted with her. But Stephanie has her hands full—a house that's falling apart, a shrivelling bank account, and some *very* strange goings-on that keep her and Ivan jumping once they're back on terra firma. There is a teenager in this story who is an absolutely priceless character as far as those of us on the LOVESWEPT staff are concerned. We hope you enjoy

(continued)

her and her remarkable role in this affair as much as we did. Full of humor and passion, **IVAN TAKES A WIFE** is a real winner!

Imagine meeting a red-bearded giant of a man who has muscles like boulders and a touch as gentle as rose petals. If you can dream him up, then you have a fair picture of Joker Vandergriff, Sandra Chastain's hero in **JOKER'S WILD**, LOVESWEPT #344. We can only thank Sandra for taking us in this story back to delightful Lizard Rock, with its magical hot springs and its wonderful people, where Joker is determined to heal the injuries of former Olympic skater Allison Josey. He mesmerizes her into accepting his massages, his tender touches, his sweet concern . . . his scorching kisses. Her wounds are emotional as well as physical, and they run deep. Joker has to fight her demons with all his considerable power. Then, in a dramatic twist, the tables turn and Joker has to learn to accept Allison's gift of love. As heartwarming as it is exciting, **JOKER'S WILD** leaves you feeling that all is more than right with the world.

Rugged, virile, smart, good-looking—that's Nick Jordan, hero of the intense and warm romance **TIGRESS**, LOVESWEPT #345, by Charlotte Hughes. What a dreamboat this sexy peach farmer is . . . and what a steamy delight is his romance with Natalie Courtland, a woman he finds stranded on his property during a freak snowstorm. The cabin fever they come to share has nothing to do with going stir-crazy as the storm keeps them confined to his home; it has everything to do with the wild attraction between them. Beyond their desire for each other, though, they seem to have nothing in common. Natalie is a divorce lawyer in Atlanta, and Nick has forsaken the world of glamorous condos, designer clothes, sophisticated entertainment, for a way of life he considers more real, more meaningful. How they resolve their differences so that love triumphs will keep you on the edge of your chair. A true delight first to last!

Ooh, la, la, here comes Mr. Tall, Dark, and Handsome himself—Dutton McHugh, Joan Elliott Pickart's devastating hero of **SWEET BLISS**, LOVESWEPT #346. When Bliss Barton wakes up with her first ever hangover, she finds a half-naked hunk in her bed! She could die of

(continued)

mortification—especially when she recognizes him as one of her brother's rowdy buddies. Dutton is not her type at all. Careful, cautious, an outsider in her family of free spirits, Bliss has kept her wild oats tightly packed away—while Dutton has scattered his to the four winds. When her family misunderstands the relationship between Bliss and Dutton, and applauds what they imagine is going on, Bliss decides to make it real. The hilarious and touching romance that follows is a true joy to read!

Fayrene Preston outdoes herself in creating her hero in **AMETHYST MIST**, LOVESWEPT #347. Brady McCullough is the epitome of rugged masculinity, sex appeal, and mystery. When Marissa Berryman literally falls into his life, he undergoes a sudden and dramatic change. He is wild to possess her ... not just for a night, but for all time. The confirmed bachelor, the ultimate loner has met his fate. And Marissa, who goes up in flames at his touch, is sure she's found her home at last. Parted by the legacies of their pasts, they have to make great personal journeys of understanding and change to fulfill their destiny to love. A breathlessly exciting love story with all of Fayrene's wonderfully evocative writing in full evidence!

I reminded you about Iris's **GOLDEN CLASSIC**, but don't forget the three other marvelous reissues now on sale ... **SOMETHING DIFFERENT**, by Kay Hooper; **THAT OLD FEELING**, by Fayrene Preston; and **TEMPORARY ANGEL**, by Billie Green. What fabulous romance reading. Enjoy!

With every good wish,

Carolyn Nichols

Carolyn Nichols
Editor
LOVESWEPT
Bantam Books
666 Fifth Avenue
New York, NY 10103

THE DELANEY DYNASTY

Men and women whose loves and passions are so glorious it takes many great romance novels by three bestselling authors to tell their tempestuous stories.

THE SHAMROCK TRINITY

THE DELANEYS OF KILLAROO

Now Available!
THE DELANEYS: *The Untamed Years*

Buy these books at your local bookstore or use this page to order.

Prices and availability subject to change without notice.

NEW!
Handsome Book Covers Specially Designed To Fit Loveswept Books

Our new French Calf Vinyl book covers come in a set of three great colors—royal blue, scarlet red and kachina green.

Each 7" × 9½" book cover has two deep vertical pockets, a handy sewn-in bookmark, and is soil and scratch resistant.

To order your set, use the form below.